DARK W

DARK WATERS

ESSAYS, STORIES AND ARTICLES BY

RUSSELL CHATHAM

WITH ILLUSTRATIONS BY THE AUTHOR

CLARK CITY PRESS

LIVINGSTON, MONTANA

Some of these stories were previously published in a different form:

"Night Moves," "Winter Steelhead," "An Angler's Afternoon," and "A Day in Paradise" in *Field & Stream;* "Innocence Lost," "The Great Duck Misunderstanding," and "Pumping Irony" in *Gray's Sporting Journal;* "Ethics," "Fishing: Mystiques and Mistakes," and "Mountain Mallards," in Aqua-Field Publications; "Shad, Rats!" and "Dessert as the Main Course" in *Fly Fisherman;* "Edward Curtis" in *Sports Illustrated;* "Sporting Deaths" in *The Co-Evolutionary Quarterly;* "Niblets: The Grand Slam" in *The Complete Fisherman's Catalogue;* "Ben Hur Lampman" in *Rocky Mountain Magazine;* "The World's Greatest Trout Stream" in *Seasons of the Angler*.

For information contact:
Clark City Press, P.O. Box 1358, Livingston, Montana 59047

For Tom, Jim and Guy,
and in memory of Ted Trueblood

In the midnight Arctic seas,
stained tropical rivers at dawn,
the Gulf Stream at noon,
where thin shafts of light
chisel down into blue-black;
a small creek in evening shade
beneath willows and sycamores;
in northern rivers
where salmon lie
in deep viridian hollows.
It is always the dark water
which promises the most.

CONTENTS

CHATHAM'S STEW: A FOREWORD

Some years ago a popular outdoor writer, his eyes ablaze, told me he was outraged that Russell Chatham had mentioned farts, belches, and women's breasts in an "outdoors" story. Who did Chatham think he was? Why was he allowed to do so? What was happening to the world?

"We all know about those things," the fellow pointed out patiently to me, in case I'd missed them, "but most of us have the decency not to mention them. And they have no place in a sporting article."

Wasn't I outraged, too?

Alas, no—and I told him so, and why not. Quite the opposite.

That story is here and another with sex acts that would have popped Jimmy Swaggart's eyeballs.

But, of course, Chatham isn't concerned with that kind of decency, which is a form of indecency, nor with "outdoor articles" as they're generally perpetrated on us. He writes with and about his passions—art, friends, enemies, eating, sport, sex, drugs, an endlessly textured universe, centered more toward the freer, western parts of America than the crowded East, where I live, which he loathes; and he does not dream to trivialize his passions by routing them neatly into separate cubbyholes. His stories are like the great stew Twain mentions at the beginning of *Huckleberry Finn.* "In a barrel of odds and ends," Huck tells us, "it is different; things get mixed up and the juice kind of swaps around, and then things go better."

A lot of juices swap around in *Dark Waters,* and things go pretty well, indeed. There is no demarcation in Chatham's life between the various kinds of life he stews himself in. He is a sensualist, a hedonist, an explorer and lover of dark waters of various stripes, a watcher and a voyeur, a fisherman, a hunter, a painter, a writer, a man who is quietly determined to pursue his own trips in his own way and to come back and tell us about them, a man (like Whitman) delighted with his own passionate diversity.

He has a passion for ducks, both the shooting of them and the feasting on them; for that wise and gentle writer Roderick Haig-Brown, (whom he met only once, all too briefly); for great meals of a dozen kinds—he seems to love describing foods almost as much as eating them; for the pleasure of fly casting and for that of swinging a shotgun on a fast bird; for fly fishing for grayling, winter steelhead, yellowtail, salmon, striped bass, in Montana, San Francisco Bay, New Zealand, the Sea of Cortés, Alaska, and in his imagination; and he is passionate about his friends. He loathes snobbishness and making fly fishing overly complex and "mindless controversies" like the one over sinking vs. floating fly lines. He brings a lot of puckish humor into the life of sport—see his delicious prescription for the use of succotash as bait for the "Grand Slam," or his account of risking a drug bust rather than disclose a honey-hole for stripers—but it is usually humor with an edge. He understands death—in the field and of friends, several of whom are movingly, unsentimentally, remembered. He likes privacy and companionship, stillness and camaraderie. Chatham is a voluptuous pilgrim, revelling in his senses.

Always there is that fullness of all things being connected, and of there being a few sensible principles to the full life. Fishing, he says,

> is much the same as painting and writing, both of which I think of as being fun. Fishing and hunting, painting and writing are all a mixture of childlike enthusiasm—fun if you will—and sharply focused energy. The successful combination of excited wonder and fierce effort produces a new sensation: satisfaction, perhaps the greatest thrill and most important goal in all our lives.

In the end, *Dark Waters* is about Chatham's satisfactions, and as such is acutely different from the bland clichés of what is called decent outdoor writing, which always dissatisfies because it is not about life but some hackneyed, safe, sterile notion of what sport should be, something untainted by farts. In *Dark Waters* you will find no bilge, no pap, little that you'd expect, feasts you'll never forget, sights and smells that only an artist's antennae could catch, shrewd sporting skills and perceptions, a lust for travel and a lust for the rich comfortableness of the known, orneryness, the lazy sensuality of the voluptuary, lots of opinions (some of them against guys with too many opinions), tough comment on other writers (some of whom I know and like or have published, or both), decency that goes far beyond conventional notions of that word. The book is bold, outrageous, wise, independent, wrongheaded, delicious, hilarious, pugnacious, and lots of fun.

That's a lot for the small price of admission.

Quite a stew.

Jump in.

Nick Lyons
15 May 1988
New York City

PREFACE

By anyone's standards this is a peculiar collection of stories, articles, essays and reviews, gleaned from a decade of working in journalism. Some of the pieces are utterly plain, while others, I see now, are deeply eccentric. All of them, however, do rather accurately reflect aspects of my temperament and character during the years from 1975 through 1985. The oldest story is "Innocence Lost," and the newest is "The World's Greatest Trout Stream." I mention this only to demonstrate, I suppose, that it takes more of a sense of humor to live happily today than it used to.

Some of the stories which have not previously been published veer noticeably wide of the mainstream hook and bullet mark. For instance, "Up Over and Down Under" was returned accompanied by the reminder that women, let alone the actual mention of sex, did not belong in a fishing story, the one exception being a caricature known among the sporting fraternity as a "fishing widow." I caught some flack on this same score when "The Great Duck Misunderstanding" first appeared in 1976. "Dust to Dust" came back to me with the editorial comment scrawled across its title page, "This is not about hunting."

I have not yet completely come to terms with Richard Brautigan's death. Some questioned whether or not there was foul play involved; most sources, official or otherwise, claim there was not. Richard was undoubtedly one of mankind's most tormented souls. Toward the end of his life even his longtime friends were literally driven away. That may have been a disguised plea for help. I'm not prepared to say.

Richard encouraged me to write from the time of our first meeting twenty years ago. He went out of his way to introduce me to several editors, and was responsible for my having a number of things published. I've never been entirely certain why he did this. He could tell I was never going to be rubbing elbows with the great Faulkner. Perhaps it was simply that he recognized in me some of the loneliness in himself. This plus the fact that neither of us would ever really be part of things, and we both loved to fish and drink.

Whatever the reason, it was good of him. I had a need to say some things, which can often be difficult without benefit of an education. I also very much needed the money, since my paintings were selling at the rate of wool suits in El Paso. Considering the thousands of hungry writers, it's quite funny to me now that I turned to this impossible profession partly as a means of generating income.

But it worked, although what seemed to me like a substantial living was really pretty laughable when viewed against the perspective of a coal miner's wages. The result was a fair amount of writing experience. I don't have any illusions about the immortality of my prose. However, I do believe that it doesn't hurt anyone, and at its best provides some entertaining moments as well as a view of life from off to the side, where I sit. Most of the work shows some evidence of my often perverse sense of humor, although once in a while disappointment and bitterness take over. This is probably part of the wrongheadedness Nick refers to in his forward. But I'm much less interested in being right than I am in owning up to the sum of my parts.

With the exception of painting, nothing in this life has held my interest as much as fishing. Fishing with a fly, a bait, a handline; I don't much care. Fishing, in my estimation, is not a hobby, a diversion, a pastime, a sport, an interest, a challenge, or an escape. Like painting, it is a necessary passion. Yvon Chouinard told me this is what climbing is for him. We agreed that to be anything less than passionate about these very personal enterprises is unacceptable. He is as impatient with the modern, cool sport climbers as I am with the thousands of yuppies who have made fly fishing one of their many activities.

So, while my two favorite things—aside from the love of family and a certain fondness for food—are sitting outside painting and fishing, my least favorites are visiting art galleries (and reading art magazines), and visiting tackle stores (and reading fishing magazines). It's no wonder I'm so often confused.

Some aspects of these stories are out of date and I have not attempted to change that. In this, they represent a time as well as a place.

The price of fishing tackle in "Winter Steelhead" tells you what it was a dozen years ago, not what it is today.

I did three or four pretty thoroughly researched articles about the striped bass and San Francisco Bay, all of them similar in nature to "Pumping Irony." I don't have any updated matching figures, partly because I have not had the time to get them, and partly because I don't believe becoming that depressed would be good for me. There are still a few bass around and hard-core fishermen occasionally catch them. Cliff Anfinson sold his boat a few years ago and I haven't been able to catch a striped bass for the last eight years, although admittedly I haven't tried terribly hard, either. It's one of the those things that's going to require more than a Bandaid to fix.

Finally, a word of acknowledgment. During the last twenty-five years I've had the pleasure of working with some very fine editors. It would be hard to assess who among them was the best. This book was edited by Jamie Harrison Potenberg, who now, as far as I'm concerned, holds that title, along with my appreciation and thanks.

Russell Chatham
June 2, 1988

THE FIELD

Duck hunting in Marin County.

THE GREAT DUCK MISUNDERSTANDING

Two drake mallards are limp on the kitchen counter. These large birds, just down from Canada, were ambushed near a marsh in southwestern Montana about four in the afternoon one still, bitter, cold December day. Regrettably, there was a third, not now present.

The slough had been stalked over several rises and through a stand of cottonwoods. There I stopped to warm my hands and admire the elegant thirty-year-old pigeon-grade Winchester Model 12 I'd just acquired, in a trade for a large painting of the Big Sur hills washed in summer light. An odd juxtaposition of places, moods, objects.

When the ducks broke from cover, jumping almost straight up and squawking, they fanned out. The first one went down cleanly. The second and third, nearly out of range, were cripples that coasted into a flat swampy field covered with a foot of snow. I found number one right away, mounted in a snowdrift exactly as he'd hit it. The others were nowhere to be seen. I began to crisscross, finally stepping on one which somehow burst up into my arms.

The third mallard died beneath the snow, becoming one of those pointless killings thoughtful hunters recall with sadness. Or maybe he tunneled his way out of Park County into another possibility with only a little lead in his foot, though it's doubtful he ever lived to hear Spanish being spoken in the towns beneath him.

Back in the kitchen the transition is being made from wild animal to something to eat. I am going to treat my new girlfriend to one of those special culinary experiences doors are locked for. She comes in unexpectedly early, while the birds are still being plucked. When she sees them she does her version of Eddie Cantor trying to blow up a truck tube, and runs into the bathroom. I lose heart and consider serving her cat shit while I have roast duck. But I already knew most people get it wrong.

My father was a sensitive man whose spirit had been utterly broken early on, and he replaced it with a shroud of ennui which effectively kept life at arm's length. His systematic self-denial only faltered when there were ducks for dinner. Duck was the only food to which he ever really warmed, and in his defense of the quality of duck as dinner, he forbade the serving of it to guests or children, neither of whom could be trusted to appreciate it. I even think the failure of his marriage was largely due to the fact his wife "didn't think ducks were that good."

It must be an inherited characteristic. When I catch trout I normally turn them loose afterward. And even when I take one home knowing it will be delicious, I'm still far more interested in catching the fish than eating it. The same with grouse, certainly a delectable bird. And so it goes with bass, salmon, pheasant. But when I see a duck, even one of those on a city-park pond that takes bread crumbs out of the palms of old ladies, the desire to kill and eat is nearly Satanic.

All game birds are exquisite on the table, but there are certain fanatics for whom nothing does the job quite so perfectly as a prime wild duck. Those on the inside often argue darkly over which species is most superb. Easterners defend the black duck; westerners, the sprig or pintail, midwesterners, the mallard. Everywhere, the tiny teal is spoken of in hushed tones. In the South, the real connoisseur will hear of nothing but the sublime wood duck.

But most people get it wrong, and so you learn not to talk about it. Raving about how you like to eat duck might bring invitations to dinner from hunters who have freezers full of them. Many of these hunters will be baffled by such enthusiasm because they themselves would "rather have a T-bone." You'll find out why when dinner is served. The missus will have stuffed the ducks with bread crumbs and baked them in a 325 degree oven for three hours, creating in the process a classic *je ne sais quoi*. Served thus, with some dried-out peas, mashed potatoes and a cup of coffee, a date with an icebox full of wet hair would be preferable.

The best way to bail out the evening, aside from very heavy drinking, is to convince the hosts the bird was delicious, and hope they'll give away the rest of the ducks from their freezer. Later they will make fun of you as a screwball, but you will have skated off with the raw material for many quasi-orgasmic moments.

I am sitting with my friend Joe in his living room overlooking San Francisco Bay. I know Joe shares and understands my love affair with the wild duck. We talk of duck hunting and duck eating.

"Let's go next door," he says. "My new neighbor is a duck-eating fanatic."

Next door it is clear that Hal, his new neighbor, doesn't trust me any more than I trust him. I am sure he uses too cool an oven, over-cooks the birds, and makes a disgusting sauce, if any. He no doubt believes I dredge the birds in flour, chicken-fry the living piss out of them, and dish them up with boiled potatoes.

"How do you fix them?" I ask cautiously.

"Roast them in a hot oven."

"How hot?"

"Five hundred degrees for about twenty minutes."

"Jesus, that's right! Use sauce?"

"Yep." Hal knows he has an audience now and stops to casually refill his glass.

"Wine sauce?"

"Wine, Worcestershire, lemon."

We fall onto the couch excitedly. His sauce is perfect, that is to say, exactly like mine. He coats the birds generously with butter and salt. He uses a very hot oven. Cooks them fast. Likes them rare. With wild rice. Wine sauce. French bread. And good wine.

Joe is giggling absurdly. He gets a shotgun out of the gun rack and tracks imaginary birds with it across the living room. Hal and I get down to some serious duck talk. By serious, I mean we are going to do it. Have a duck dinner together.

The problem is that duck season has been closed for eight weeks. A Long Island duckling or any other market duck is as much like a wild duck as a twelve-pound self-basting turkey is like a mourning dove. We could use frozen birds left over from the season and trust that they've been treated properly. Hal admits having two sprig. Joe has three teal. This little piggy has none.

Trade, that's it, trade somebody something for one. How about a nice fresh striped bass for a mallard or two? My brother still has ducks in his freezer and yes, he says he would like to have a bass.

I know a place to catch one and the following evening I'm fly casting into the teeth of a spring gale, waiting for the first feeders. The first one comes almost to the boat before the hook pulls loose. With an easy flip of its tail I see a plump mallard glide out of sight into the murky waters of the bay. The wind gets stronger and my chances of not hooking another fish are steadily improving. Surprisingly, a bass surfaces near shore, and in a quick backhand maneuver I cover him and he's on. This duck puts up a good fight but is no match for the ferocity with which I haul him over the transom and make him mine.

When you consider the great cuisines of the world, notably those of the Orient and France, many of the finer dishes are made with duck. In a sense, duck is to chicken what pork is to veal. It has extraordinary texture and flavor.

Because of their fine qualities, ducks have been domesticated for centuries. In France the two most commonly raised for the table are the Rouen duck and the smaller Nantes duck. There are several other varieties, including a crossbreed used especially for foie gras. The Rouen duck is unique partly because of the way it is killed. In order to be sure the bird loses absolutely no blood, it is smothered. Because of this the blood remains distributed in the meat, giving it a reddish brown color and a special flavor which is highly valued. These ducks are eaten the day they are killed to avoid a possible buildup of toxins.

Wild ducks are found in the Orient, but there, too, the birds were long ago domesticated and thoroughly incorporated into the cuisine. For instance, in the north, ducks are sometimes inflated with air so that the skin lifts away from the flesh to become very crispy, creating the famous Peking duck. In the south, ducks are often filled with seasoned liquids, then roasted to create Cantonese duck. The Chinese roast, simmer, braise, smoke, steam and deep-fry ducks. The results are universally sublime: the aforementioned Peking duck, roast-honey duck, chestnut-braised duck, red-simmered duck, eight-jewel duck, white-simmered duck, Nanking duck, duck steamed with tangerines, steamed deep-fried pressed duck, stir-fried duck, tea-smoked duck, and hundreds of variations on these recipes.

The French have their famous *caneton à l'orange* and variations thereof, duckling mousse, duckling with cherries, olives, turnips, sauerkraut or peas, and the remarkable *gallantine de caneton.* But perhaps the duck's finest moment in classic French cuisine arrives in the form of *caneton Rouennais en salmis à la presse,* described by the redoubtable Paul Bocuse as Rouen duck from the Hôtel de la Couronne, and of which he says, ". . . it is the best one can imagine." Essentially, this is a roasted duck, carved in the standard French manner, served with a sauce made in part of the reduced juices pressed from the bird's carcass. This dish is guaranteed to make you forget all about the farmer advancing across his barnyard, pillow in hand.

All of this exotic and sophisticated cookery notwithstanding, a wild duck remains a wild duck. The reason why domestic and wild birds are so unlike one another is very simple. Domestic ducks walk slowly around the barnyard, and are generously fed so their meat lacks density and becomes laden with fat. In the United States, the ducks which best demonstrate this are the Long Island ducklings available in markets. Wild waterfowl are all migratory. They travel thousands of miles at high speed. It is said that the reason ducks and geese fly in a "V" formation is that the strongest bird leads and the others follow in his slipstream. When he tires, one of the birds which has been traveling toward the rear moves up to take his place. These waterfowl suggest the vast scope of seasonal mysteries through a tremendous display of grace and nobility.

The heart is the only other muscle which must sustain longer and more even activity than the breast of the wild duck or goose. For this reason, the breasts of these birds are very large, rich with life-giving blood, and extremely dense, the birds themselves being almost entirely without fat. Wild goose, incidentally, is also totally unlike its domestic counterpart. No other table bird has as much fat as a barnyard goose. Wild goose, like wild duck, has none. Therefore if you follow a recipe for domestic goose while trying to cook a wild one, you'll ruin it.

As with other dark-meated birds and animals—sage hens, doves, antelope and deer for instance—very precise cooking is essential. Oven temperature should never fall below 450 degrees and cooking time is short. Mere minutes too long and these meats will be dried out and ruined. All game, especially wild duck, should be cooked rare. If you don't like it you should stick to gruel or corned beef hash. A friend recently pointed out that waitresses in the sleaziest diner in America always ask how you want your steak cooked. You might say in this case it's a toss up who is more ignorant, the fry cook or the customer. In a truly fine restaurant, never is the diner asked how he would like something cooked. That is the chef's job.

In Europe, game is available in most good restaurants. Chefs there have centuries of experience to inform them and they never get it wrong. In America, it is unlawful to sell game of any kind and so it remains the hunter's reward alone. Here, the chef who must get it right is you.

I call Joe. "Got some ducks. When can we do it?"

"How about this Thursday night? That'll give us time to think about it for a few days, you know, *to get ready*. I'll call Hal because he'll want to leave work early that day."

On Wednesday I am in San Francisco looking around some of the galleries when I run into a woman I'd met almost a year earlier. We were at a party and she had taken me home. She was a musician and in her apartment a cello leaned against the Steinway. I had thought of Casals passionately instructing a young female student to "hold it like it was your husband." Was I going to be her cello?

She was so fully ripe a woman, with such an important frame, that there was nothing to do but whatever she might ask. She came right to the point, telling me to get undressed and wait for her in bed. In that zone of half-consciousness we all recognize as the result of too many drugs I began to wonder if she was crazy and if so was she also dangerous. I heard voices coming from the bathroom. Perhaps, I thought, she is talking to herself before slashing her wrists, or worse, planning to bring razor blades to bed. When I peeked through the door she was naked and had a green parrot on her shoulder and they were talking. When it got light she had woven me into a cocoon of sexual heat that stupefied me for weeks.

Now, a year and half-dozen fruitless phone calls later, we are sitting having a cappucino and her voice is deeper than I remember, her hair darker red. When we are about to part she says simply, "Be at my apartment at nine tomorrow night. Ciao."

"Joe listen, there's this woman . . . well, what I was wondering was could we possibly do the duck thing on Friday night."

"Are you kidding? You're kidding, aren't you? Hal would short circuit. The ducks are thawed! We've been *getting ready*."

8

"But I . . . you're right. What am I saying? I'll be there."

On Thursday I make an ingredients run. You can't trust anyone else to do this. First stop is the Sonoma Bakery on the town square in Sonoma to purchase the San Franciso Bay area's finest loaf. The French salesgirl drops the magnificent two-pounder into the bag and it hits bottom with a sound like hands clapping.

Next stop is Petrini's in Greenbrae, one of the great supermarkets on earth. I buy two-dozen fresh bluepoints, large perfect avocados, two grapefruit, fresh lemons, parsley, shallots, garlic, unsalted butter, Worchestershire, red currants, red-currant jelly, a dry red wine for the sauce, and at the deli counter, a good brie.

In Sausalito I find two bottles of Echézeaux and a Pommard, old, heavy, aromatic reds that seem just the thing to go with the duck. And a bottle of Cordon Bleu brandy. I have a handful of dry bay leaves from a tree near my mother's house, and from the Ramy Seed Co. in Minnesota, a pound-and-a-half of extra-long-grain wild rice.

When Joe and I get to Hal's his lady is putting on her coat. "I don't want to know anything about this," she says, backing out the door. Hal explains that she saw it before and was appalled. His ducks are sitting on the sideboard. From his wine rack he has taken two bottles of Châteauneuf-du-Pape and they are standing open. I open my bottles and we begin to examine the ducks, counting wounds, guessing ages, noting the peculiarities of each species. We have a mallard, two sprig, three teal, and two wigeon.

We dress up the bluepoints with a dash of Tabasco and lemon juice. They are light and fresh, perfect with a bottle of Fumé Blanc which just happened to be in Hal's refrigerator. The bay outside the window looks like modern art, shiny and pinkish in the afterglow of a smooth spring day. Two canvasbacks swim by and I undress them in my mind.

The beginning of our sauce is the end result of a previous meal. A stock was made by simmering duck carcasses with vegetables, and was then frozen. Now it will be heated and reduced. We drop in a couple of the bay leaves.

"What the hell do you think you're doing, Hal?"

"I'm going to stuff the ducks with this onion."

"I knew it. Joe, he's going to ruin the goddamn ducks."

"Trust me. I stuff them loosely. Little salt and pepper. Little on-

9

ion. Little butter. Splash of sherry."

"Okay. But make mine extra loose. And for God's sake, when you put them in the oven don't let the ducks touch one another."

We bring the wild rice to a boil twice, rinsing it each time. The trick is to cook it more by soaking in hot water than by actual simmering. Brought to a boil for the third time, in chicken stock rather than plain water, it is removed from the heat and left to stand. I make a small salad of avocado slices and grapefruit sections, finishing it with a vinaigrette dressing.

We turn the oven up to 500 degrees. Before roasting, the ducks must be completely and heavily covered with butter softened to room temperature. The birds are then salted and put on a low rack set on a shallow roasting pan.

Timing will be crucial, so it pays not to drink too much until the birds are cooked, carved and served. The three big ducks go in first, followed seven minutes later by the wigeon. Six minutes later the three teal go in, and ten minutes after that all the ducks are done. When the ducks come out of the oven, Hal and I carve them carefully into two halves, disjointing the wings and legs from both the carcasses and the breast meat. These are set on a warm platter.

Meanwhile, Joe has added to the stock a dash of Worcestershire, a bit of finely-chopped shallot, and several squeezes of lemon juice. The stock is boiled rapidly for some minutes to develop its flavor and also reduce it a bit further. Finally it is strained into a skillet, brought to a fast simmer, and the carved duck placed skin side up in it to take the blood-rare edge away from the carved face. We are careful not to leave the birds in this stock more than about ten seconds. Hal has a wonderful kitchen utensil not much in demand around the suburbs these days: a duck press. The halves of duck are placed on a covered, heated platter, ready to be served. The carcasses are then pressed to extract every bit of juice, which is then added to the reduced stock. We add some pre-soaked currants, and the sauce is done. Finally, the French bread is toasted under the broiler, rubbed with a garlic clove, and liberally buttered. We are ready to eat.

Before long, rice and sauce cover the table. Lemon wedges lie scattered about. French bread is torn loose. Each bite of rare, juicy meat is a new thrill, wild duck being something like a cross between filet mignon and fresh deer heart, only with more flavor than either.

Our wine glasses become increasingly grease-smeared as we pick up each carcass and suck it down to bare bone and gristle. We carelessly gulp the fancy vintages. Our shirt fronts are ruined. Juice and blood run from elbows onto knees and the floor. The room is blurred. We belch, fart, laugh and groan.

As the carnage winds down I think about my date and wonder if it's too late, but the face of the clock refuses to come into focus. I find a mirror and what I see reflected there can only be described as soiled.

I grab a glass of cognac and flop into a lounge chair out on the deck. The salt air feels good and as I gaze vacantly into the middle distance, nearly comatose, I wish without much conviction that her tits were in my eyes.

SPORTING DEATHS

The report of a high-powered rifle shattered the silence of the autumn afternoon. In his camp, a hunter was surprised by the nearness of the shot, and more surprised still to look up and see his partner walking up to him.

"You see a deer so close to camp?"

"Nope."

"Why'd ya shoot?"

"I dunno."

"Whatcha shoot at?"

"Pussycat."

"What?"

"A pussycat I said."

"What the hell . . ."

"I shot a pussycat and we gotta get outta here."

"Jesus Christ, I don't . . ."

"Know the people got the Winnebago over by the crick?"

"Yeah."

"Cat belonged to the kid. He ran out after he heard the shot and found the thing all blown to hell."

"For God sake why . . ."

"I dunno, I dunno. But we better move camp 'cause the little brat ran back to get his folks an' he was cryin' an' yellin' Daddy, Daddy, somebody just shot my pussycat."

One winter a number of anglers were fishing for steelhead in a certain pool. This pool was large and still and green and in its protective depths lay many fine fish waiting for rain to swell the river. Soon one of these magnificent rainbows took the bait of one of the fishermen, but in the early moments of the struggle ensnarled another's line.

"Fish on!"

"Hey! I got one too!"

"I think you got my line."

"Bullshit!"

"Whaddaya mean bullshit? Yer line got crossed with mine after I got hold of this fish."

"We'll see who's crossed with who when we get this sonofabitch on the bank."

"Yeah, if we ever do with you pullin' on my line!"

"Here he comes now, take it easy."

"Okay, slide 'im up on the gravel."

"Watch it! He's loose! Grab him!"

"Got him!"

"Phew!"

"Biggest one I've caught all season."

"You caught! Why you . . . that's my fish an' you know it!"

"I don't know no such thing. Hooks come loose before we could see fer sure an' I hooked him first."

"Give 'im here."

"Hey! You bastard, put up that pistol!"

"Not unless you gimme my steelhead."

"It ain't yers."

"All right fellas, let's settle this peacefully now. I'm the warden here."

After hearing the arguments of both parties the game warden took out a skinning knife and divided the object of the debate down the middle, handing a half to each contestant.

On a blustery, snowy fall day on the Yellowstone River I'd gone out hoping to catch brown trout, but hadn't been able to. After a while a two-man yellow life raft floated into sight upstream. The fisherman in it was furiously casting a dry fly at my bank.

"Gettin' any?" he inquired as he neared.

"No."

"I am. Been doin' real well."

"That's good."

"You usin' wets or dries?"

"Wets."

"Better switch to dries like me. Dries is how you get 'em. In fact, there's one now!"

His rubber raft swung around and around out of control as the fish he had just hooked darted about.

"Looks like a good one too! Uh oh, wait a minute, why it's a goddamn whitefish. You a whitefish fan?"

"What?"

"Are you a whitefish fan?"

"I don't know what . . ."

"Good! I hate 'em!"

With that he hurled the unfortunate whitefish as far up the riverbank as he could and continued on out of sight. After a brief search I found it wedged between some logs, gasping spasmodically. I carried it to the river and held it upright in the current for many minutes until it could hold its own. Then it swam out of sight.

One summer I was walking with an uncle and cousin along a foot trail in the Los Padres National Forest. Presently we came upon two men walking in the opposite direction, who could well have been a pair of latter-day Pancho Villas. Indeed, our trailmates sported the sort of arms one might expect to encounter during a Latin America revolution. The men wore knives, pistols, canteens, belts of cartridges crisscrossed over their chests and carried rifles with wood all the way up to the muzzles, such as were used in many an early campaign.

"How's fishin'?" asked one.

"Not bad. How's the hunting?"

"Terrible. We ain't had nothin' but a few sound shots."

I went to school with a boy who had a vague interest in hunting and fishing. Now, when we occasionally pass on the street or happen to meet by chance in a bar, small talk passes between us on those subjects. I remember a story he told one night after we'd had quite a few.

"Ever hear of the Black Pearl?" he asked.

"I don't think so."

"Worth a fortune."

"Oh?"

15

"Yeah. You find 'em in oysters."

"Hmmmmm."

"Me an' a friend of mine have been lookin'."

"What?"

"The oyster company. There's millions of oysters behind those fences."

"You don't mean . . ."

"Minus tide at night. Last week we were sittin' there and must've had a pile of open oysters big as a car. Guy's dog started barkin' an' lights started goin' on in the shacks. Jesus, we barely got outta there."

"A close one, eh?"

"Yep. But it's worth it for the Black Pearl."

"How many have you found?"

"None."

On a bright, clear November day some of us were fishing for steelhead in a pool called Watson's Log. Somewhat upstream is a place known as the Narrows. There, two or three men were fly casting and presently one of them hooked a fish. Otherwise there hadn't been much doing, so right away a few onlookers gathered. As the fight continued a veritable gallery hovered behind the fortunate angler. Speculation arose over the fish's possible identity, with the majority favoring an especially large king salmon. Some thought it might be a striped bass. Soon the huge fish wallowed helplessly far out on the surface of the pool.

"Look at the size of 'im!" someone cried.

"What is it?"

"Can't tell, but it's sure a whopper."

"Good Lord! It's a carp! He's hooked in the tail!"

"Ugh!"

"Look at the size of that ugly bastard!"

"Ooh, hoo, what a giant!"

Then the massive bottom feeder was dragged high and dry and someone bashed in its skull with a heavy river stone. The fish would have weighed more than thirty pounds and was a leviathan of its kind. Only prejudice makes us think carp are ugly; they are actually beautiful and golden. The Japanese portray them with long sensuous brush strokes. By December after the ravens and seagulls had finished, only a vague skeleton and a few dollar-sized scales remained.

One day not long after I was out of high school, I found myself in a car with a casual acquaintance, headed for some lakes near where we lived to go trout fishing. Suddenly, as I was looking out my window at the scenery, the car began swerving and jouncing so that my head hit the roof. Finally, we came to a stop in a ditch among the sagebrush.

"What happened?" I asked.

"I saw a rabbit and tried to get him."

A friend of mine had always wanted to go elk hunting. After much planning and anticipation the day arrived when he left for the long-awaited pack trip into Wyoming. A few days later I got a call from him.

"I'm back."

"Back?"

"Yes, I'm home."

"But I thought . . ."

"So did I. Three other hunters and myself packed on horseback into a remote area. Mules carried our supplies and we had two guides. The first goddamn morning we're there this one dude blasts the guide right off his horse. Deader'n hell. So we draped the poor bastard over his saddle and rode back and that was my elk-hunting trip."

One winter day a bunch of us were standing around on the bank of a priceless little steelhead river in northern California. It was a river I'd visited since I was a boy, and the topic of conversation was the tragic decline in the fishing. About then an old gent who'd been working the pool below us hooked a nice steelhead. We all turned to watch him play it. Soon my companion offered a speculative remark to the crowd.

"I wonder," he said, "what you'd do if you knew that the fish you just caught was the last one in the river?"

And someone answered, "Whap!"

These stories are all true, and I could go on. Their merit or interest lies not in their credibility but in their morbid irony. I fish and hunt with more than average frequency, always have and probably always will. Yet there are times when I seriously wonder why, especially as far as hunting is concerned wherein success is irreversible. But somehow, when the phone rings and a friend suggests going duck hunting, I'm always enthusiastic.

Death has always loomed large in my concept of nature and the outdoors. And I don't necessarily mean to restrict that comment to the philosophy of the survival of the fittest or food-chain biology. One of my earliest memories is walking up the canyon from our ranch with my father. At one point quite far from the house we sat down among some willows to rest. As I recall it now, my father had his shotgun along and shot a crow as it landed in the branches above us. More than that, I remember a steep bank nearby which rose directly up from the creek bed. For some reason my father began explaining how to get home if anything should happen to him.

"Always follow the crick," he said.

Somehow I got the idea that he was going to die, which was why he was explaining how to find my way home. I began to cry. There was really no reason for it, but even today the memory of those minutes comes back sad and stark and real.

My father showed by example how to be careful with guns and he had rules for their use. I could take a gun out alone but never with another boy. Two boys together were liable to become excited and careless.

"Think how you would feel for the rest of your life if you shot someone," he would say. "When you're by yourself there's only one person you can shoot."

And pistols were never allowed.

"Too easy to accidentally point at someone," he warned.

Guns are made to kill; that I learned long ago. So while I very often admire a particular firearm for its beauty, I know at the same time whatever aesthetic properties it possesses are strictly peripheral to its real purpose.

When I think back upon my life of sport, the deaths and near deaths stand out. I fish more than I hunt, and in fishing the matter can be simply avoided by releasing the catch, which I most often do. It's hard to release a deer that's been slammed by a 180-grain hollow point.

A variety of hunting successes sticks in my memory. Once on a walk with the .22 when I was ten or eleven I saw a cottontail rabbit dash into a thicket. I looked in and saw him sitting right there looking back at me. His innocence occurred to me as I shot him point blank.

Too ashamed to admit what I'd done and stunned by the cruelty of it, I left the rabbit in there, walked home and put the gun away for many years.

Then there was the time I armed myself with a slingshot. This wasn't your average forked stick cut from a tree branch, like my father had made for me years before. This one, bought in a "toy" department, was advertised as a weapon. Which it was. One afternoon among the bay trees I spotted a gray squirrel. I was right beneath him, so I could see clearly the little lead ball whistle between his spread hind legs as my shot barely missed. I was seized by a sudden pain in my own groin at the thought of a hit, and at the same time felt the utter relief of a clean miss. It was like waking from a nightmare in which you'd just committed a murder to find yourself innocent.

When we were young a neighboring rancher shot an eagle with his deer rifle. After showing it around he threw it down a shallow ravine near the road. To this day the spot is known as "where so-and-so threw the eagle." My grandfather had a buckshot still lodged under one fingernail when he died, all that remained of the time a careless quail hunter caught him with a load of no. $7^1/_2$'s. How many gut-shot deer ran to die in a remote creek bottom somewhere? A crippled mourning dove's liquid eye stares from a head covered with the most indescribably exotic, tiny pinkish feathers, the head soon to be bashed against the breech for mercy's sake.

The media often accommodates here, too. In the pages of a sporting journal a hunter sits with his buck. He is in the snow, which is extensively bloodstained, alluding to the gore surrounding the capture of this trophy animal. On television an archer stalks a grizzly. This unsuspecting member of an endangered species is feeding on a carcass as the arrow slams into its chest. The animal's death, duly filmed, was so pathetic that I cannot describe it.

The other afternoon I went grouse hunting. I'd had a nasty experience the week before, when, after a friend had shot and crippled a bird, I picked it up and cracked its head over a fencepost, then left it while we hunted. When we came back an hour later the bird was sitting looking at us. I nearly vomited at what I'd unwittingly done, and quickly broke its neck. But this incident had faded into the past as they all do and again I was walking in the woods.

A half hour had passed without a bird when suddenly a shadow flushed overhead. I raised the shotgun instinctively, only to see a blue jay. During my motion I'd pushed the safety off and before I knew what I was doing I'd touched off a shot. A few feathers flew and the jay swerved unnaturally into a nearby tree. I couldn't believe what I'd done. This was worthy of a nine-year-old and I was horrified. For a moment I hoped the jay was unhurt but I knew too well that he was hit somewhere. My dog raced aimlessly around the woods confused since she'd flushed no grouse nor seen any fall. My other dog, a completely useless Basenji that I'd just taken along for the walk, stood by and whined. I walked over to the tree and looked up at the jay who stared down, his beak half open. Several times I walked back from the tree thinking he'd fly away, thereby absolving me from the consequences of my hasty actions. But he didn't as I knew he wouldn't, because he was shot. Standing back, I pointed the gun at him for long minutes, then touched off another blast. At this he fluttered from the tree and flew over my head where I jerked off another crazed shot, missing him completely. This last can only have been part of some demented effort to be "sportsmanlike." By now I was in shock, the dog was racing more feverishly than ever about the woods trying to figure it out, and the Basenji whined even more loudly. The jay landed in an aspen, very wounded. I began to sob uncontrollably. Walking close, I aimed and with my fourth shot blew the thing to kingdom come. Laying down the gun, I cried for some time, then sat quietly in the late autumn afternoon, listening to the sounds in the woods and watching the light change as it glinted off the Yellowstone River in the far distance.

I'm a hunter and a fisherman, always have been and always will be.

Why?

MOUNTAIN MALLARDS

A Plain Discourse
on Duck Shooting
in the Rockies

The official opening of duck season always seems inappropriately early. This is especially true in the northern Rockies, where the first week in October is usually warmed by Indian summer. It isn't out of place, then, to look forward to a rather personal opening day which may not arrive until the first of November. If you're somewhat indecisive anyway, and anything less than a fanatic about duck shooting, October offers plenty of other field sports to divert your attention: upland bird hunting for pheasants and five species of grouse. West of the divide add quail and chuckar. Steelhead near the Washington-Idaho border. And in the late fall, trout fishing, the best of the year.

It's hard to predict when the first real cold will hit the Canadian prairies, freezing potholes and putting birds in the air in long, uneven strings aimed south. It doesn't happen all at once. Ducks, in common with other migratory creatures, sometimes move for reasons not easily detected or understood. There will come a day, for instance, when I step outdoors in Livingston, Montana, and sense fall in the air. Ordinarily this will be in late August and I won't be able to explain precisely what it is I feel, but it is there. Animals must surely feel these pivotal changes with a good deal more clarity than I do. Ducks, in their thoughtless serving of ancient instinct, simply blast up out of the pond, climb to three thousand feet and hold at a steady forty miles an hour, following the bright ribbons of rivers far below.

Let's say this personal opening day starts in the afternoon because I haven't gotten up early enough to organize a dawn hunt. It is snowing intermittently with the wind gusting out of the north. The general deer

21

and elk seasons have just opened, thus diverting hunting pressure; it seems a perfect time to privately open the waterfowl season, which has been open to everyone else for several weeks.

The initial hunt involves walking around a tract of land of perhaps fifty acres, laced with potholes, ditches and a small, winding spring creek. There are bound to be some mistakes. One happens immediately when four mallards jump out of the stream near the car, well before I've loaded the gun. I tense, imagining that this late and futile gesture will prevent it from happening again.

The first spot that normally holds a few ducks is a tiny spring at the head of a slough, hidden well in the cottonwoods and rich with watercress. I calculate a wrong turn and end up in a wild-rosebush thicket, staring at a confused cottontail. I back out, go way around and come to the spring as if by surprise. There are no ducks. While I stare blankly at the water as if something might crawl out from beneath the cress, two mallards that have been sitting off to the side jump and squawk, keeping a cottonwood between us as they climb out fast.

The next stop is an open pond, with some good cover for a sneak. I peer carefully through the trees and underbrush and see about a dozen birds on the water. At a distance they are at first hard to identify; closer they top up, scoot around, and distinguish themselves as green-winged teal. It's necessary to crawl the last little way to get within range. Once there, I look cautiously through the chokecherry and see the birds well bunched up. I stand abruptly to make them fly; the ducks blast straight up, then flare away, catching the wind. I manage to isolate one on the rise, elevate above it and drop it cleanly. It is the only one.

I walk along the creek, alternating in and out of cottonwoods and pines. It's too windy to be able to hear ducks talking but beyond the trees an occasional single or double circles, looking for a resting place. At the edge of a clearing I stop and watch. Most of the birds are very distant, coming into sight above the dark mountains. One comes beating straight toward me. There is little time to decide whether he is within range or in the foolishness zone. I opt for the former and swing up behind the fast-moving bird, which pulls way out in front by ten, maybe twelve, feet. It is a long, sweeping grandstand play, the kind I hope works in spite of everything. Luck has it and the dead drake mallard soars a hundred yards into the creek.

The next two holes are empty so I make the circle back to the car.

22

There is perhaps an hour-and-a-half of shooting time left and I want to set out some decoys on a pond about a mile away. There is no real way of approaching the pond under cover, and the bunch of mallards floating on it flare. They circle once, wanting to drop back in, but I'm too far from the underbrush to run for it and crouch like a lummox with my bag of decoys. The ducks wing on up the valley.

Six or seven decoys are enough, partly because more than that are hard to carry, and partly because on these little creeks and ponds using more than a dozen is pointless. There are no massive flights here, as along the major flyways. I've seen singles, doubles or sometimes small flocks of eight, ten or twelve birds looking for a place to drop in and rest.

In the wind the decoys sit taut at the end of their tethers, swaying slowly back and forth. The blind is a space in the chokecherry bushes about twenty yards from the pond. Theoretically, birds should be taken at the ideal distance of twenty to forty yards, as they set to come in, pass over for a look-within range, or flare up and away.

The first two ducks to come over don't realize this. The loud whistle of their wings is heard only seconds before they fly directly overhead from behind, getting out of range at once. The next bird follows the script more closely. A drake mallard drops in, wings set and wavering, like a high looping softball pitch coming to the plate. I stand, let him start to flare and he drops into the decoys.

The next bunch is more interesting. First seen at a distance, they circle widely, staying in sight. When they come over for a look I attempt a high-ball call which comes out sounding more like Zoot Sims than I hoped. They seem not to have heard from upwind because they veer, pick up speed and begin losing altitude. Ordinarily mallards are not this forgiving when hooted at inanely. I tuck the call away, thank God for small favors and resolve in the future to stick to the more innocuous feeding gabble. When ducks come in like this they are nearly always traveling faster than is apparent. Or else their angle of descent is deceiving, because I poke two neat holes in the sky while the ducks move on unruffled, if not entirely unnerved.

It is nearing the end of shooting time. Mallards move well at twilight hour and this evening is no exception. Birds begin coming in with regularity against the wind. There are the always mysterious misses, and finally, two more mallards down to make a limit. As I go out to

23

pick up the decoys, a distant sound is borne in on the wind, one which takes some moments to register. It always sounds a bit like dogs barking far away or people talking in the next room. Even when I know full well what it is there can be a recognition lapse.

A line of Canadian geese is coming in unseen below the cottonwoods. Ten seconds, twenty seconds, and then I see them against the sky and know at once they must pass directly overhead. They are within shooting range and I huddle under the decoy sack, afraid to move. Geese within range always look far too big, like the letters in a first-grade reader. I'm not specifically hunting for them, and don't get that many chances to see them in range. These are coming on like B-29's, with the wind. Overhead their talking is very loud, the wing beats clearly audible. The trick with geese is to lead the head and not the body and to remember, again, that they appear to be moving slower than they really are.

I have plenty of time to think about these things before it's time to raise up. I take the lead bird before he is upon me and hear the shot hit. He wavers but doesn't fall. The second shot is right overhead and the goose collapses, hitting the ground with a terrible thud. Opening day is over and I couldn't have diagrammed a better one.

I never really get used to seeing ducks high in the northern Rockies. The first glimpse of them strung out above a jagged rimrock of the Absaroka Range reminds me of the strange gargoyles in the *Wizard of Oz* that come down from the witch's castle to attack Dorothy and friends. The birds find sanctuary in this harsh landscape down in the river valleys and in spring creeks and ponds. Such relief is relatively scarce compared with the vast expanses of open, dry prairie and sharp, high peaks, and the birds must naturally follow a course which keeps them in view of places to feed and rest.

At this latitude the Rockies divide the central and Pacific flyways. Hunting, then, is marginal by other standards. The big flights of geese hold to the east where there are more open fields. The sprig travel farther west, guided by the coast itself. The bulk of ducks at the headwaters of the Missouri or along the Yellowstone above Billings are mallards. With the exception of large flights of goldeneye late in the season, the sighting of most other species is remarkable.

Ducks begin to appear about the first of October after the early storms sweep across Canada. After that, sportsmen start thinking about putting the trout tackle away, buying ammunition, and making appointments with the service station to have their cars winterized.

I sometimes arm myself as a hyphenate, putting the shotgun over my left shoulder and the fly rod over my right. Usually I end up with neither ducks nor trout. There I am, waiting in the blind for an hour with nothing going over, watching a trout rising just past the decoys. I give in and step forward with the fly rod, and moments after putting down the trout with a nervous, clumsy cast, two-dozen mallards flare away in panic as I foolishly rush back to the blind.

Finally, Indian summer breaks and the cold sets in for good. Trout fishing is still a possibility but one's attention turns more firmly to the ducks and geese which show in more impressive numbers. A good duck day now will not be confused with a good trout day. Of course, a big game hunter might want to torment himself with that particular conflict, but that's another story. Wing shooting is wing shooting and with the best upland bird hunting past, shotgunners can pretty much keep their special form of schizophrenia in hand.

A good duck hunter must be jealous of the places he shoots. The reasons seem obvious enough. The birds should be able to work in a natural pattern, undisturbed. It is, after all, rather a game and I want to be able to call the birds and pick my shots according to my own temperament and not someone else's.

The best way to hunt mallards, or more accurately, the most interesting way, is to blend jump and decoy shooting. Mallards move best at dawn and dusk, and in between I can usually work out some sort of walk by which to jump them out of ponds, potholes or ditches. I can do this after an early morning decoy shoot, or in the afternoon before setting the decoys out for the evening flight. Pass shooting— walking the river and taking the luck of the draw, as it were—is usually the hardest way of filling a limit.

It takes time to learn how to call but the practice is worth it. One of the first things to keep in mind is that you want to sound as unlike Zoot Sims as possible, even if you do like jazz. Good duck calling is not a tremendous mystery. You need to know basically how and when ducks call one another, and you need a good call and good call technique. The only way to learn is to hang around with someone who knows how to do it properly, then go out and practice. A good rule of thumb: if it sounds funny to you it sounds really funny to the ducks.

Once there is any snow on the ground the matter of visiting favorite duck water incognito is vastly simplified by use of the Sheet Ploy. A simple bedsheet wrapped around him makes the hunter largely invisible even to the most suspicious of ducks. A KKK outfit is ideal but these are not available from Eddie Bauer. Ask your wife for a throwaway bedsheet. You want an old-fashioned plain white one. Those with pictures of Arnold Schwarzenegger on them or floral patterns won't do. When your wife wants to know what it's for, tell her you're going to disguise yourself as a snowbank.

Don't be discouraged if your first experience hunting with the Sheet Ploy doesn't work out exactly right. Aside from feeling like a fool, you may have trouble getting settled in a way that will let you spring into action without becoming hopelessly tangled in the sheet. You may feel like a gunfighter in a full-length raccoon coat.

Let's say I have six decoys floating in a likely pond. Above the horizon a large flock of mallards is coming right in, wings set, rocketing down from a thousand feet. I peer at them from under the sheet, feeling like a vigilante. When they are on top of the decoys I make my move, but I am standing on the critical edge of the sheet and manage only to topple over backwards. Still hoping for a shot at the terrified ducks, which are climbing out of there as fast as possible, I raise the gun and the wind blows a corner of the sheet up over my eyes.

But let's assume I manage to make a version of the Sheet Ploy work. Now I'm on the back porch, both hands full of ducks. A surprising number of hunters lose interest at this point. Some say picking the birds is too much work, others lack any interest in them as table fare.

It may perhaps be a matter of some opinion, but wild duck is one of the most superb game meats in the world. If you like steaks well done you might as well stop reading right here. Eating a well done steak is not unlike eating an alarm clock. You won't like a properly cooked duck either. As for the amount of trouble involved in cleaning and picking the birds, well, anything worth doing requires some effort. Picking ducks, for example, is a lot easier than cleaning manure out of a Swiss watch.

Unless you hunt the southern part of the range where weather is apt to be a bit on the warm side, ducks are best hung. Where weather is always cool, as it is in Montana, five days is about right. Clean the birds but leave them feathered. The purpose of hanging is to tenderize as well as help develop the flavor. In the mountain states fishy puddle ducks are nonexistent. All the birds feed on grain and corn and are universally sweet tasting.

Wild duck has less fat than the leanest of fillets. Therefore, the main error to avoid in preparing them is overcooking. An overdone wild duck is loathsome and inedible. Never confuse a wild duck with a domestic duckling. The latter may be as much as fifty percent fat, and it is greasy fat which can only be removed by cooking the bird a long time. Optimum cooking time for a large mallard is about seventeen or eighteen minutes if the bird is at room temperature, and about twenty to twenty-five minutes if it is cold. You may want to adjust the time a few minutes this way or that to suit your own taste but always use high heat: 500 degrees for roasting, and close to that temperature with a covered barbeque. Before cooking, the birds should be liberally coated with softened butter.

If you have filleted the birds first into halves consisting of breasts and legs, and plan to sauté them in butter and vermouth or something like that, the same rule applies: do it hot and fast. A minute on each side uncovered, then a final minute with the vermouth and a cover should be plenty.

Stuffing the birds loosely with onion and celery will go a long way toward removing any slightly unpleasant taste. Don't count on this however, if the ducks are distinctly fishy. The best solution to that problem is to get a different duck.

Garnishes, sauces and accompanying dishes may be as varied as the number of chefs who prepare them. Whatever these turn out to be, any meal of wild duck is a special treat, special enough to make even the most resolute complainer forget about how frustrating it was to pull those pinfeathers, or how cold the pond was as it came in over the top of his hip boots when he reached for the prize.

Russell Chatham and Richard Brautigan fish Armstrong Spring Creek.

DUST TO DUST

Late one night in the fog, just before Labor Day of 1984, upstairs in a hollow old summer home in the northern California beach town of Bolinas, the author Richard Brautigan let himself have it with a .44 magnum. What was left of him was found four or five weeks later because, according to the papers, when he failed to arrive in Montana for the hunting season, worried friends up there called the Bay Area and sent someone over to check out his house.

I was a friend of Richard's for nearly twenty years, which was long enough to have watched him shoot to smithereens any number of unlikely items including an entire wall of his Montana home, clocks, telephones, dinnerware, sport jackets, and, his favorite target, television sets. It was enough to make me feel downright effete for shooting at the stars from the yard of my house just a few miles away.

In any case, during all the years I knew him, both in California and Montana, I can never remember him going hunting, or even talking much about it except in passing. Once he presented a gift of a sixteen-gauge double-barreled shotgun to Jim Harrison, inscribed "Big Fish," to commemorate a four-pound brown trout Jim had landed in the Yellowstone River, but that was it.

The word "macho" appeared in the postmortem press just as it so often does when journalists turn in a report on a man reputed to like the blood sports, and who happens to live someplace other than in a condo or co-op apartment on one of the Dream Coasts.

Webster gives macho a certain amount of negative weight by defining it as, "A virile man, especially one who takes excessive pride in his virility." Interestingly enough, there is no correlative word which unflatteringly describes the female who is feminine and who "takes excessive pride in her femininity." Even the archaic term feminie, which means womankind (especially the Amazons) is largely meaningless to us. The closest female equivalent of machismo may be what some modern women—secretaries and shop girls in particular—refer to among themselves as femme femme. This term describes a woman who is preoccupied with feminine sexuality as well as perhaps the coy and stereotyped behavior usually listed under the heading of the Feminine Mystique. Unlike the obviously macho male who is scoffed at by nearly everyone, the femme femme woman is disliked only by bull dykes, resentful spinsters and certain humorless members of the clergy. This is true even in San Francisco where the board of supervisors recently declared the three-dollar bill legal tender.

The media, with the exception of that small part of it devoted specifically to the blood sports, tends to view hunters as people of imperfect character; macho, overly competitive boors who are boisterous, boastful, uncultured, rude, insensitive and violent.

The sad truth is that probably eighty percent of those who go afield with a gun or rifle fit the above description. These people aren't hunters in any true sense of the word. They're gunners trespassing in the woods under direction of some very suspect motives.

One often hears, especially from non-hunters, that men confuse their guns with their penises. This has never happened to me, and so it seems absurd, something like confusing your nose with a car wash. The confusion might have been started years ago, the first time an army recruit mistakenly referred to his rifle as his gun during boot camp, and the outraged drill sergeant made him parade around the grounds with his rifle in one hand and his dick in the other, repeating over and over, "This is my rifle, this is my gun, one is for fighting, the other's for fun."

In a similar vein, psychoanalysts love to make inferences and draw conclusions by relating real events to hypothetical ones. For instance, a friend of mine told his therapist he had always wanted to make love to his aunt. The doctor explained what that really meant was he wanted to make love to his mother. "No I don't," my friend replied. "My mother was a dog. My aunt was beautiful. Nobody in his right mind would want to screw my mother." So much for Freud.

Richard Brautigan was not a macho man. He was unyielding and often infuriatingly obtuse, but he had a certain defiant dignity and great

personal strength because of his strict literary convictions. At the core
he was essentially fragile and sensitive in a society which tends to reward those virtues with poverty and an early death.

The California ranch my great-great-grandfather established during the 1860's is part of what was once an enormous Spanish land grant
in Monterey County. In an odd way, it's a curse to have been born
and raised in one of the most sublime places on earth. I've been around
the world and have never seen another place of such sensuous, languid
character, or where the climate is so benign.

From the ridges above our ranch house, on a clear day, you can
see Salinas and Monterey Bay. Up there the sea breeze is always surprisingly fresh and its voice is soothing as it sweeps across the tall yellow grass and through the sorrowful, scattered oaks.

Down in the canyons, on the flats beside Chupinas Creek, it is
always warmer. In August and September it can be very hot, and that's
when my father and I went dove hunting.

During the Depression my father said there were a great many
birds. He sometimes shot thirty in an afternoon with relative ease. By
the time I started going along, which was soon after the Second World
War, we were very happy with ten or less.

We walked around the hayfields looking for birds on the ground.
We never shot them there, you understand, but this was how we found
them. You could see them bobbing and strutting, while they fed for
quite some distance, so there was always suspense as to whether they
would hold long enough for us to get within range before they flew.
Sometimes we were surprised by doves jumping up out of the creekbed,
or out of a patch of tocalota weed. Or else there were singles or doubles
simply flying by, wings whistling on an erratic, swerving course. My
father was a good shot, and he didn't often miss.

Hunting dogs have no fear of the sound of a shot; the noise itself
suggests the excitement of the hunt, creating a demeanor of extreme
happiness. A gun-shy dog often cowers even at the sharp clacking of
a shell being chambered into a pump gun. This timidity, or caution—
call it what you like—can be genetic or due to remembered trauma.

I was a cautious, rather timid child, yet the sound of gunfire didn't
frighten me. I cannot recall even hearing it. My recollections of hunting
in those formative years concern the smell of sage and tocalota, the

forlorn, soft sound of the mourning dove in the distance, the song of the quail, again in the distance, the odd, rather rhythmic cries of the red-headed woodpecker, breezes rattling the dry oak leaves, the silent circling of buzzards, the muffled tinkling of the creek's diminished rif- fle, the afternoon sun diffused through the sycamores, the presence of my father just beside me, or else whistling his familiar whistle behind a stand of trees. I saw birds sometimes falling, but I never heard the shots.

This notion occurred to me when I recalled the first time I ever discharged a firearm. We weren't hunting, but there was still the simple distraction of place, and being with my father.

Several things about the incident make it easy to recall. The first was we had a giant bag of fireworks illegally procured for us by our Chinese housekeeper. Second, it was the only time I ever recall being in the vicinity of the Mission Dolores, a district of San Francisco where only Mexicans were supposed to go. We had gone there to borrow a .45 automatic pistol from a serviceman my father had met. The war was over, but it still carried tremendous weight as an immediate, his- torical, exotic event. The man was a captain and my father informed me sternly, "We are going to shoot the captain's pistol."

We drove down the coast to what is now Pacifica, shot off all the fireworks (mostly giant firecrackers), and repeatedly fired the captain's pistol from the cliffs down onto the beach below. If you've ever shot a .45 automatic you know how powerful they are. And if you have ever lit an old fashioned four-inch Chinese firecracker, you know how loud they are. Do you know what I remember about that afternoon? Seagulls hovering on the breeze and the sun glinting off the ocean. I remember only peace, quiet, and happiness.

My father's first rule of hunting was, "Never point a gun at any- thing you don't intend to shoot." His second rule was that I could only hunt alone because, "That way there is only one person you can shoot accidentally." He meant this in reference to peers, naturally, not adults. The second rule was inviolable.

If you shoot something when you are alone, there is never any secondary reason for it, no pointless sense of competition or triumph. You must deal realistically with the act itself. An easy shot can some- times appear difficult to someone else, and the temptation is to keep quiet.

I wasn't allowed to take the shotgun out by myself, only the .22; therefore real bird shooting, which is to say dove or quail on the wing, was out. So, I had bluejays, magpies, crows, cottontails and squirrels. Dove and quail were fair game if I could get one on the sit, but this was ethically complicated because only a poor sport shot those birds when they weren't flying. It was much better to save them for "real" hunting.

In order for the emotional tension to be fully stressed and functional in a real hunting situation, it is necessary to understand and love your prey with a force precisely equal to your desire to kill and eat it. The business of emotional tension rides on a sliding scale, with the desire to hunt and kill rising and falling due to any number of variables. The question of honor is important as well. To kill anything without an apology is unconscionable.

Doug Peacock, the grizzly bear expert, told me he survived numerous attacks or "rushes" from grizzlies by holding his ground, averting his eyes and cowering slightly. Aggression or flight would both have been fatal. The desire to shoot certain birds or animals is heightened by their flight, and dissipated by their immobility.

Speed and stamina are two of the qualities that make certain gamebirds and animals exciting to shoot, but excitement alone, uncomplicated by regret, becomes a negative, like the word macho. Neither is such a crime, really, merely flawed character in the latter case and a sign of a one-dimensional mind in the former. Neither is like child molesting.

I went on a controlled pheasant hunt in California recently. As we were uncasing our guns, a young boy, hunting nearby, accidentally shot the man who had taken him out. I saw how it happened and it was clearly not the boy's fault. The kid became hysterical, and was largely ignored in the confusion that followed. The man didn't die, but it was close. The boy had not been instructed on how to use the gun, and the man foolishly and carelessly stepped in front of him to flush a bird which was being pointed by the dog.

There were many reasons for the accident, all of them having to do with lack of proper teaching. The boy didn't know exactly how the gun worked physically, and he was not prepared to deal with the excitement of the flush or the ease with which the trigger could actually be pulled. Most of all, because of the casual, commercial, obvious, easy way these birds were dumped in the field only to be harvested hours later, he had no reason to adopt an attitude of wonder, reverence and respect for the incomprehensible mysteries of a real hunt. I suspect that boy will not want to hunt again for a very long time, if ever.

Richard Brautigan's last published book was called *So The Wind Won't Blow It All Away*. It is, in part, about a family who sets up a living-room group of furniture on the shore of a lake.

> *I had become so quiet and so small in the grass by the pond that I was barely noticeable, hardly there. I think they had forgotten all about me. I sat there watching their living room shining out of the dark beside the pond. It looked like a fairy tale functioning happily in the post-World War II gothic of America before television crippled the imagination of America and turned people indoors and away from living out their own fantasies with dignity.*

It is also about how he, Richard, accidentally shot and killed his best friend with a .22 while out pheasant hunting.

> *"What happened?" I said, bending down to look at all the blood that was now covering the ground. I had never seen so much blood before in my entire life, and I had never seen blood that was so red. It looked like some liquid flag on his leg.*
>
> *"You shot me," David said.*
>
> *His voice sounded very far away.*
>
> *"It doesn't look good."*
>
> > *So The Wind Won't Blow It All Away*
> > *Dust . . . American . . . Dust*

I love you Richard, and although hunting has saved my life more than once, and I don't want to go on without it, I understand perfectly why you wanted to shoot Sonys rather than roosters.

HOME

Roderick Haig-Brown

RODERICK HAIG-BROWN

Observation, Ethics and a Real Good Time

By August the idea of going to one of the spring creeks again for trout fishing was beginning to get me down. And the Yellowstone, in spite of its formidable reputation and official blue-ribbon classification, is a moody, tricky stream, one which has suffered tremendously at the hands of thuggish fishermen who ply its waters with live bullheads and are openly contemptuous of bag limits and the conservation ethic. I mean to take nothing away from the delights of trout fishing. It's just that I felt a compulsion to get out of Livingston, Montana—the alleged "Trout Capitol of the World"—and over the divide and into Oregon, Washington or British Columbia, to see some rivers flowing west into the Pacific. Not that I have anything against New Orleans; quite to the contrary. But that's another story.

If you think about going fishing in the Northwest, the most logical starting place from a literary point of view is Roderick Haig-Brown. So there in the Yellowstone Valley, in the vague warmth of what passes for summer in the Absaroka Range, I took his books down from the shelf to be reread, and stacked them in two neat piles on the edge of my writing desk. In one pile: *The Western Angler, Return To The River, A River Never Sleeps, Fisherman's Summer* and *Fisherman's Fall*. These were the ones directly concerned with where I was planning to go in September, the ones which would specifically set the mood for the fishing I would do. But I gathered together in another pile the rest of his works I had been able to lay my hands on, and would read them again, too: *Fisherman's Spring, Fisherman's Winter, The Living Land, Starbuck Valley Winter* and *Measure of the Year*.

After *The Western Angler* and then *Fisherman's Fall,* my enthusiasm to reach the coast was vastly renewed. More than that I looked forward to another stop in Campbell River for a visit with Haig-Brown, having compiled numerous mental notes about topics we hadn't had time to talk over the previous fall.

But throughout the month of August a check was not in the mail. It failed to appear during September as well, until finally I went back to trout fishing, and then grouse hunting, in a childish, surly, self-pitying funk, going afield in a globe of irrational remorse and longing. In the evenings I took Jack Daniels firmly by the throat, picked up Haig-Brown, and ossified myself while imagining doing something that mattered. Like fishing for salmon.

Further reading of the marvelous books did little to alleviate this greener-grass syndrome. As autumn slid by, offering a stupefying banquet of reds and golds and crystalline days, my admiration of Haig-Brown's work increased and became laminated layers of hope, remembrance, and promise. My second visit with this justly legendary man became an ever more exciting and imperative prospect.

It may have been Ezra Pound who said something like, "There's no problem an artist has which can't be solved by the application of a few bank notes." All too true to form, what stood between me and western Canada was the condition of my bank account, which in sober moments suggested rather strongly that a stretch in debtor's prison rather than a fishing trip lay somewhere in the not-too-distant future. As I said, the check was simply not in the mail.

Finally, late in October, having watched fall evaporate, I kicked the last scant evidence of fiscal responsibility right in the pants, closed out the liability I called a checking account, impetuously borrowed some money, and headed west. Nothing on earth seemed quite so important as seeing Haig-Brown, and later catching the steelhead and possibly the chum salmon run in the lower Nimpkish River.

Soon after I got the news: Roderick Haig-Brown had passed away earlier in the week.

On the first of November I was looking at a long tidal flat on the coast of Washington just a few miles below the Canadian border. It was one of those opalescent forenoons which seem to demand you be on the water. Ordinarily, this should have been a rather grim, rainy season of the year, but the day's broad tints of hazy blue layered back toward the horizon, suggesting anything but sorrow or death. The pungent smell of smoke from the mills came in across the bay on a gentle breeze, but any symbolic objections one might have had about that were out of place. If I couldn't believe in living the fullest possible life today, I thought, I was probably out of luck.

"If one has to die, I should think November would be the best time for it," wrote Haig-Brown in 1944. "I should think there is nothing very bad about dying except for the people one has to leave and the things one hasn't had time to do. When the time comes, if I know what it's all about, I suppose I shall think, among other things, of the fish I haven't caught and the places I haven't fished."

Ten yards out from where I waded, a cutthroat swirled. A quick cast and he was on, a fish of perhaps two pounds, bright and vigorous. Bank one sin of omission avoided.

A few days earlier it had been raining and I had spent some time walking along a small stream full of spawning cohos. Many were already dead or dying. I have fished for salmon all my life and their cycle forms a perfect paradox: they have come to spawn and inevitably die, yet they are as magnificent in their being as they will ever be.

Haig-Brown wrote:

Once I pitied the salmon in this state. Now I love them. They are death itself in a shell of life, but that remaining shell of life, though without hope or reason beyond the safety factor it provides, is impressive. . . . I see them now on the shallows near my house, often two fish together, slowly forced down by the current, turning fiercely against it as it presses on their broad thin flanks and warns them of their weakness. It is the sort of thing man has glorified in himself as the undying spirit of man. Seeing it here so clearly, long after purpose and hope have gone, I can recognize it for what it is: the undying spirit of animals. I find it no less admirable.

To some people the thought that the salmon, all Pacific salmon of all species, die very soon after spawning is a depressing one. They see in it only decay and waste, and sort of pathetic frustration of life. This is a natural view, but it does not question deeply enough; the end of the salmon is not death and corruption, but only fall, the autumn of their cycle. . . . As the winds stir and drift the dying

41

leaves, so the waters drift and stir the dying salmon against the gray-brown gravels of the stream beds. But under those gravels life is strong and secret and protected in the buried eggs, the real life of the race. . . . In spring life will burst from the gravel as it bursts again from the trees, into the massive yield of the new cycle. Death is seldom more fleeting or more fertile than this.

In the history of English-language angling literature, one would be hard-pressed to find a more fundamental, explicit or spiritual model for expanding and enhancing our lives through the sport than the books of Roderick Langmere Haig-Brown. His bottom line concerns turn out to be reason and ethics, based upon lengthy, keen observation; all the result of his profound love for the natural world. He might rightly be called a nature writer, for all his books, including the novels, involve the outdoors in one way or another. But unlike so many of the others who, while addressing their audiences from behind the often pompous facade of three names, never get beyond sentimentality, partiality of spirit and decadence of style, Haig-Brown clearly transcends the genre. His work, as Arnold Gingrich pointed out, "is universally negotiable as literature."

Haig-Brown is a writer first, a fisherman second. Perhaps second is a poor choice of terms—he is a fisherman as well and he comments on this rather succinctly.

It is fashionable to call any occupation that does not contribute in some dull way to the world's material wealth an "escape." It is a ridiculous fashion, as little connected with reality as acute insanity. . . . Reality for any properly constituted man in a properly constituted society can never consist solely in materially productive work. A balanced and rounded man who is really living a life instead of enduring it, will have many interests beside his work, and they will all be part of his reality. Sports like hunting and fishing, actively and positively followed, are an important and integral part of living for many men. They are not escape from problems or work or reality, but are complementary to the more ordinary, and often less exacting, routines of living, giving substance and meaning and rounded form to a life that would otherwise be a monotonous passage through some seventy years of the world's history.

*Like the hunter, the hawker and the fowler, the fisherman takes life
in finding his pleasure. It is reasonable to ask of him that he make
it as keen and thorough and satisfying, as productive of growth in
himself, as he reasonably can. For only then can it be the strong and
sensitive pleasure of a civilized man.*

*Fishing to me is not, as some of my critics have suggested, a way
of life. But it is one of the keenest and best-wearing pleasures of life.
. . . . Men may be raised differently, under different philosophies,
with different needs and different values. But hunting and fishing
are only less universal than hunger and love and death.*

*I remember a sympathetic left-wing friend once wondering what would
become of me in his revolution. "A writer," he said musingly. "Well,
I suppose a writer is a producer in some sort of way. Or is he?"
Feeling the liquidation squad close behind me, I said boldly, "Producer, hell. A writer's a natural resource."*

The fine weather persisted and I took advantage of it by fishing
the Nooksack River, in which the cohos and cutthroats were running.
On those clear days you could see well into the craggy mountains of
Canada, now topped with snow. I had wanted to go over to Vancouver
Island quite badly, but somehow it seemed more correct not to. I was
where I wanted to be. It was no accident.

Early in the novel *Starbuck Valley Winter*, Don Morgan faced a
decision: to go to work in the sawmill like so many others, or to go
out on his own, trapping and fishing. Referring to the fishermen and
trappers he knew, Morgan thought:

*There was something different about men like that, and they seemed
more important than men like Bill Staple, the yard boss down at
the mill, or Buck Hansen, the head sawyer, or even, maybe, Mr.
Ross, the superintendent. It was being your own boss that made the
difference, making up your own mind about what work you'd do
and how you'd go about it. . . . The trap-line idea had been in his
mind. It seemed to solve everything; instead of a job in the sawmill
it would mean a winter in the woods; instead of a batch of monthly
pay-cheques that couldn't possibly add up to the price of the Mallard
by the time fishing started, it meant any possibility you liked to think*

*of, from losing your grubstake to the price of two boats like the
Mallard. Best of all it meant being free in the Starbuck country
instead of tied down to a millyard under a boss.*

It is easy to forget that the risk of losing one's grubstake is one of
the conditions of being free. I had certainly chosen to forget it back in
September when all I could do was whine about having to shoot grouse
and fish for trout instead of being able to take a long, expensive salmon-
fishing trip. It had been so many years since I made the decision to be
an artist, and henceforth to never take any other job, that I'd forgotten
how good it was never to have to kiss a single undeserving ass. I had
blamed my lifestyle for cheating me out of a last visit with Haig-Brown
as if I were bolting solenoids on Chevrolets in Detroit at gunpoint, my
two-week vacation eight months away.

Haig-Brown never wrote with a message, and says so on the last
page of *Fisherman's Spring* "This book has no message, and heaven for-
bid that I should wish one on it at this late stage." Earlier in the same
book he is more positively specific: "To entertain, in its highest sense
of providing sustenance for the mind, is the most important purpose a
writer can have." But throughout Haig-Brown's work there is a certain
implied message, or, more accurately, an invitation, for he never insists. Descriptions, explanations and suggestions are generously and kindly
offered and you find that the essential agent is pleasure.

Happily absent from his writing is that boorish, tiresome stance
of the "expert" giving his boring advice on how we might catch more
fish or kill more game. Instead, Haig-Brown observes and informs purely
for its own sake, and he does it with astounding clarity, a complete
lack of hysteria, and no sense whatsoever of personal gain. He invites
you to enter his world, and it is not so much the rather specific world
of the fisherman as it is the broader, richer one of natural cycles, of
wonder, gratitude, and most of all, hope.

And if you are a fisherman, and most will be who read Haig-
Brown, you will find yourself described in his work not as a loafer and
purveyor of false tales, but as a thoughtful, responsible, vigorous, often
poetic citizen. "Fishermen are searchers. It is true we search for fish, at
times with great diligence. But we search also, as men always have, for
experiences; and there are no greater experiences than the seasons, varied and repeated year after year in our special comings and goings."

ETHICS

You take the high road and I'll take the low road
I'll be in Scotland afore ye.

OLD SCOTTISH BALLAD

Several years ago we were fishing the north fork of the Umpqua River for summer steelhead. On this tradition-bound stream most fishermen use the greased-line technique, and it is indeed a fine method. But during our trip, most of the fish seemed to be holding in the deeper pools. We naturally switched to sinking lines, a move which allowed us to catch and release quite a few nice fish at a time when others were doing little more than complaining.

Later when we stopped at the store to buy some gas, I was surprised to hear the owner berate one of my friends by accusing us of "bothering" the steelhead by using "immoral" lines. My friend, novelist William Hjortsberg, was stunned at first and then began to laugh. He had never met an angling snob before, and aside from the obvious question of how catching a fish on a floating line fails to bother it, delivered this bemused rebuttal: "Immoral! How can a line be immoral? Only people are immoral. A line is just a line!"

Every facet of life seems to have its share of discrimination and prejudice. Ludicrous as it may seem, fishing is no exception. Those of you out there who fish with sinking lines are considered little better than grave robbers by the floating-line purist. It wasn't so very long ago that the country's most famous fly fisherman flatly stated in the leading outdoor magazine, "Fishing with a sinking line isn't fly fishing." This is like saying brushing your teeth with a stiff bristle Py-co-pay is doing something else but that an Oral-B 40 is the real thing.

How can this sort of purism be viewed as anything other than semi-fascistic nonsense? It is pointlessly totalitarian and hopelessly intolerant, a materialistic fetishism not based on the quality of the fishing at all.

45

But, the purist counters, it's better to catch fish on a dry fly than on a wet fly. This is precisely the same as saying aspens are better than firs, fine gravel is better than large boulders, chairs are better than tables, apples are better than oranges. Fretting over whether tarpon fishing is harder than salmon fishing, or whether dry fly fishing for brown trout is more dignified than catching them on streamers, will spoil your fun. The matter of relative difficulty attributed to various kinds of fishing has gotten out of hand. When people talk of The Challenge, saying they are matching wits with the trout, are they suggesting they are as stupid as the fish? You can balance the brain of the biggest trout in the world on your thumbnail. How would the smartest brown trout in the Letort do against Bob Verini on *Jeopardy*?

Let's go back to the business of the greased line and the sinking line as they relate to steelhead fishing. For summer-run fish the floating line is more efficient. In a word, it is easier. A competent angler floating a line through a riffle is a lot like Mom running the vacuum cleaner along the windowsill—if there's a dead fly there she'll get it. So why all this snobbishness manifested in stores called shoppes, handmade Scandinavian sweaters, or hooks with upturned eyes forged in England? Why not just simply say, "I fish this way or that because I like it."

The whole rather mindless controversy over sinking versus floating fly lines is like a debate over which is better, radio or television. The answer is not the same for everyone. With regard to the former, you hear and imagine. With television you hear and are shown. Fishing with sinking lines is something like listening to a play on the radio. You visualize what is happening by imagining it. Fishing with a dry fly, or, say, on the shallow flats in Florida, is like watching TV: if you are imagining things you are doing it wrong.

The matter of ethics or morals, no matter what the activity, has nothing to do with objects. As an angler, you may be fitted from the tips of your toes all the way around and out to the tip of your rod with the finest and most expensive gear that Hardy Bros. has to offer and still turn out to be a bum sport. Think about it.

NOTES ON BEN HUR LAMPMAN'S *A LEAF FROM FRENCH EDDY*

This is not a book about horse racing. On the contrary, it is, as its cover states, "A Collection of Essays on Fish, Anglers & Fishermen."

If Lampman's prose style appears at first to be dated, and just a tad more flowery than need be, well, that's because it is. In the long run, though, these mildly regrettable lapses are worth overlooking because of the otherwise clean and simple armature upon which they rest.

This is not a book which will particularly appeal to the angling snob, that denizen of urban and suburban life who is forever on the prowl for newer and more correct tackle; ever alert, while visiting acceptable and popular waters, for others of his kind so that he might negotiate an opportunity to sidle up, casually remove his briar, and with forced nonchalance inquire, "Seen Ernie?"

To wit:

As for me, I have no patience with trolling, and though I consider fly fishing to be the poetry of angling, I find the most substantial prose of this consoling diversion to be in bait fishing. It is true that the troller often catches the larger fish, and the compensations of a changing scenery and a superior deftness remain to the fly fisherman; but for the more solid satisfaction of fishing I greatly prefer the gentle eddy and the waiting rod. There is a captain of police who esteems

47

himself a fly fisherman of parts, and whose inclination toward that
sort of angling has even progressed so far that he captures luckless
bugs and ephemera along the water courses, and, bearing these home
with him, contrives very passable imitations thereof in wool, and
silk, and the feathers of orient fowl, as the jungle cock. Such he
swears by, and mightily, for it is true they will entice fish, quite as
a scrap of red flannel, impaled on a hook, will bring a hungry trout
flashing to the surface . . . but I regard him as a genial fellow gone
somewhat astray, and as one who has befooled himself that there is
merit in deceit . . . he has lost forever the very amiable odor of
driftwood fires in a slow rain, which it is the habit of bait fishermen
to kindle while they await the strike . . . my friend has, or so I
believe, so hedged himself about with dogma, with form and cere-
mony, that he has quite lost the true flavor of his favorite sport, and
is as inextricably snarled in his own delusions as a hook in a tangled
creel.

In one sense certainly, *A Leaf from French Eddy* is an ode to the
flaneur. We so often forget while living this modern life with all its
convolutions, its considerable inertia and excess, its incessant hype, that
the simplest and most easily accessible diversions are still so often the
best.

Lampman was an essayist who happened also to be a journalist.
What seems pertinent about this in contemporary terms (remembering
that Lampman's career began in 1912 in Gold Hill on the Rogue River
and continued thereafter at the *Portland Oregonian*) is that his work is
marvelously abstracted away from the lowest common denominator.

In large part, Lampman's work addresses itself to a concern for
ethical behavior. In one essay he talks at length about the superb beauty
and grace of trout, then touches adamantly upon the need for quick and
merciful dispatch thereof, and finally urges "a straightaway disposal of
them as insures the minimum loss of color and charm and utility."

He chastises fishermen who do not take care to immediately place
their catch in cool, moist ferns and grasses. "It is not within the scope
of lawful authority to refuse such fishermen their licenses to take fish,
pending their penitence, conversion and reform, but certainly it is that
they show themselves unfit to bear the state's warrant for the capture
of trout. Ethically all trout belong to fishermen that love them well,

and quite as ethically is it true that fishermen who do not love the fish they take, but take them only for the excitement of the moment, to dishonor them afterward, are in point of fact merely poachers upon the riffles and pools of their betters."

Unprepossessing as it may at first seem, this book offers refreshing counterpoint to the self-indulgence of so much of today's outdoor writing. And if Lampman's work never quite ascends, as did Roderick Haig-Brown's, to that point where it is "universally negotiable as literature," it does serve to point out that work clearly within the genre can still be utterly delightful.

NOTES ON EDWARD S. CURTIS' *KUTENAI DUCK HUNTER*

We did not think of the great open plains, the beautiful rolling hills, and winding streams with tangled growth as wild. Only to the white man was nature a wilderness and only to him was the land infested with wild animals and savage people. To us it was tame. Earth was bountiful and we were surrounded with the blessings of the Great Mystery. Not until the hairy man from the east came and with brutal frenzy heaped injustices upon us and the families we loved was it wild for us. When the very animals of the forest began fleeing from his approach, then it was for us that the Wild West began.
LUTHER STANDING BEAR, SIOUX CHIEF

There is no more complete and viable record of a culture at peace with the natural world than the volumes of photographs of American Indians by Edward Sheriff Curtis. In his poetic yet powerful *Duck Hunter*, the figure, much as in a Sung Dynasty painting, is an observer rather than an intruder. He is an integral part of the scene, topically and formally, the parts as inseparable from each other as the black and white shapes of the oriental yin-yang symbol. Curtis saw his subjects with the heart and clear eye of the true artist. As a painter and draftsman as well as a photographer, he attained art's greatest goal: he made his process invisible. Thus we are able to enter the very lives of his people.

Today as we survey a largely ruined environment, many are now looking back to the Indians hoping to discover a philosophy to replace the "Man Against Nature" one we've been using. It is important to note that Curtis' hunter carries no visible weapon, nor are there in fact any ducks in the picture. Yet the mood is explicit. This man is *waiting,* which in one sense is the largest part of any sport afield.

The reproductions of duck-hunting scenes hanging in corporate offices, put end to end, would probably reach around the world. But this vast example of artistic industry may be little more than vice, empty commercialism feeding a fire of non-specific desire to become part of something sensed but not genuinely understood. The difference between the duck hunter Curtis shows us and a lithograph of an orthodontist drawing a bead with his Model 12 on a two-dimensional canvasback is precisely the difference between a culture with a long tradition of spirituality and one without.

Like all art which sticks, the implication of the subject matter is what provides the hard core of the work. There is surely an age-old pocket in the subconscious which triggers sympathetic human response to the unexplainable phenomenon of migrating animals. Perhaps it is simply a kind of proclamation that there is, after all, an order to things. Ducks are one of the many creatures that provoke this sense of wonder and gratitude in us. Curtis has given to us the Indian's legacy of spirituality in a form we can see and, much more importantly, feel. If we commit ourselves to learning that man and nature are one sacred entity, we will have gone a long way toward improving our own condition and that of the earth on which we live.

Black Elk talks of cycles:

> *Everything the Power of the World does is done in a circle. The sky is round, and I have heard that the earth is round like a ball, and so are all the stars. The wind in its greatest power, whirls. Birds make their nests in circles, for theirs is the same religion as ours. The sun comes forth and goes down again in a circle. The moon does the same, and both are round. Even the seasons form a great circle in their changing, and always come back again to where they were. The life of a man is a circle from childhood to childhood, and so it is in everything where power moves.*

THE NEW FLY

"Look at this! It's a new fly pattern I just invented."

"Hmmm. What . . .?"

"I call it Wickersham's Sea-Diving Pancake Thriller."

"Who's Wickersham?"

"Oh, he's just the guy who discovered that striped bass carry genetic-memory genes, that's all. The guy who, if indirectly, has made the classic book on fly patterns, *Lies* by I. M. Aphool, instantly out of date. Who's Wickersham, indeed!"

"Oh."

"Let me give you a for instance. Some of the bass that live in San Francisco Bay at Hunters Point had great-great granddaddies who spent the winter in Monterey Bay. Follow me? The old boy used to gulp squid down there and they were the best things he ever tasted."

"So?"

"So! You're not getting my drift here. The kid, who now summers at Hunters Point, remembers those squid through a process called genetic-memory transferral. That's why, as anyone can tell you, the bass at Hunters Point are suckers for exact squid imitations. Take a closer look at the Pancake Thriller and tell me what you see."

"It looks like a potato chip."

"Exactly. I made it by dipping chicken feathers in Crisco and then deep frying them. Let me tell you how it happened. One spring day Philo Wickersham was shad fishing on the Feather River when a boatload of kids tipped over in the riffle just upstream from him. One of the things they lost was an open bag of potato chips. As the chips passed Philo he could see young striped bass picking them off. Now, Philo forgot about this incident until one day, just last week as a matter of fact, he was sitting in his skiff on the Berkeley Flats. A school of bass surfaced nearby and he tried everything in his fly book: sardine, mackerel, mullet, anchovy and pinfish streamers, solid-gold and sterling-silver hooks, a spreader rig with five flies all of different lengths, a squid pattern (the kind that works so well at Hunters Point), an eel fly and a hot-pink shrimp fly. Nothing worked. Discouraged, he slumped in his seat and took out his lunch while the frustrating bass continued to swirl all around him. He couldn't eat and angrily tossed his lunch into the bay. The bag of potato chips in it broke open and the bass went wild. Wickersham gazed forlornly and helplessly at the rampaging fish knowing he had stumbled upon the very school of fish he had watched in the riffle up on the Feather, and that they were total suckers for a well-presented potato chip. Look as he might, there was nothing in his fly box that would do the trick. In a word, Wickersham got the horse collar simply because he didn't have the right fly."

"You mean the Sea-Diving Pancake Thriller."

"Exactly."

NIBLETS:
THE GRAND SLAM

Dear Mr. Chatham:

One recent evening down at our local tavern, a friend told me that canned corn made good fish bait. Is this true? Any help you can give me on this subject will be appreciated.

Henry (Hank) Applebaum
Lincoln Center, Kansas

Dear Mr. Applebaum:

Yes, I can confirm that canned corn kernels may be used as bait. They make good chum, too. And since your question lies a bit outside my main field of interest, I'd like to accompany my reply with a suggestion that you address a similar query to Homer Circle (a fishing editor, not a group of ball players with four baggers to their credit, as Ed Zern once thought).

The use of corn is familiar to all writers. We use it most frequently to dupe weakminded editors or strafe innocent laymen. In these cases its use is probably best described as chum, though occasionally a sucker is actually caught.

You are not the first to be confounded by corn. During the late forties I used to read a comic book called "Colonel Corn." I was ten years old before I realized the word colonel wasn't pronounced like it was spelled. So you see, I was had by corn at an early age.

But to move along to your question. Corn makes fine bait, having many advantages over other conventional types. In the Rocky Mountains, for example, fishing for whitefish is a popular winter sport. Maggots are the favored bait. Some of the locals save rotting carcasses and during thaws probe the festering depths to get enough of the white larvae for a day's fishing. In very cold weather the maggots are held in the mouth to keep them from freezing. Hold them long enough and you can create your own hatch. (But that's another story.) I ask you, would you rather have a mouthful of writhing maggots freshly dug from a skunk's stinking spleen, or a teaspoon of Green Giant Niblets?

Which brings us to the use of succotash in lakes where there are more than one kind of fish. Say you want to go for the *Grand Slam*. That is to say, catch four kinds of fish at once. Succotash is your answer.

Weekend fishermen may be satisfied with a canned product but this will never do for the very avid. For one thing, the traditional recipe calls only for corn, lima beans and string beans. As the home-run simile implies, four baits are required, and carrots get the nod. During tournaments where the competition can get pretty stiff, hard-core anglers lightly salt and simmer fresh ingredients, but frozen or canned vegetables can be used in a pinch. Most consider the actual bait far less important than the terminal tackle.

Start with your lima bean. Cut off one end and carefully dish it out slightly with a baby's silver egg spoon. Using light green size-A Nymo thread, tie the lima—it should be a nice plump one—to a number-six popper hook.

Next comes your carrot. Those who use fresh veggies score a real plus at this stage. Leaving the carrot raw (or boiled only enough to make it just slightly flexible), put a hole through it lengthwise with an ice pick or similar tool. Slip a ten-foot piece of twelve-pound leader material through the hole and tie to it a number-one treble hook.

On separate leaders and hooks (Eagle Claw bait-barb types are best) impale your string bean and your corn kernel, leaving the leaders randomly long.

Rig the four baits on a stiffish boat rod as follows. First put your string bean on a twelve-foot dropper. Six feet behind that tie your corn hook on a three-foot dropper. At the end of the line itself (which may be braided monofilament of at least eighteen-pound test) attach a swivel. To the swivel tie your prepared lima on a four-foot leader. Trickiest of all is the carrot: its leader must be exactly eight feet long, affixed to the main line precisely one foot behind the twelve-foot string bean dropper.

You need a float. Any kind sufficient to maintain the surface will do. It should be fastened to the main line at the swivel. The last time I tied up this outfit I used a cork from a bottle of '63 Richebourg, which I drank during rigging up.

Now you're ready to go fishing. Take the boat out to the middle of the lake (the middle is as good of a place to start as any). Carefully lower the four baits over the side, avoiding tangles. Keep your eye on the float and row slowly away to a distance of about fifty feet.

Your lima bean, if it was properly prepared, should be barely visible four feet behind the float. The corn, carrot and string bean will be hanging straight down from the line on their droppers; the latter, hopefully, on or near the bottom.

Now you must wait. Your first strike comes on the string bean, probably a carp or sucker, though you hope for the catfish necessary to begin the *Grand Slam* correctly (aficionados dip the string bean in a mixture of warm pork fat and ox blood to improve their luck in attracting Mr. Whiskers).

When you have a bite, set the hook. Put the rod in a holder or other secure place and begin rowing steadily toward shore. The corn kernel will dart erratically and make itself irresistible to a nice fat crappie or bluegill. Either of these beasts will hook themselves.

As you continue on, the struggles of the bream will attract a pike. Remember, your carrot is on an eight-foot dropper which should allow it to wobble within a foot or so of the struggling sunfish. The pike will hit the carrot first, thinking it is another small fish.

As you near shore, the struggles of the three captives will cause the lima to pop along the surface much like a baby frog. A bass will take it in shallow water.

Beach the boat and reel in your *Grand Slam*. There is no official recognition available from the Field & Stream contest, but it should be reward enough to know that only a small handful of anglers, largely in the British Isles, have ever accomplished this difficult feat.

One final point: the use of corn, other vegetables, and even dairy products provides an advantage for the elderly on fixed incomes, the poverty-stricken and anyone else otherwise disenfranchised, since they may purchase their fish bait with U.S.D.A. Food Stamps.

Tight lines!

Russell D. Chatham

FISHING:
MYSTIQUES AND
MISTAKES

Perhaps all you can say is that there are great lapses or discrepancies in time; that and the simple if inexplicable fact that some people have fishing in their hearts.

In some ways fishing has Gone Modern, although it's a good way behind the injection-molded consciousness of skiing, or almost any other sport you can name. I for one am not complaining; some nineteenth-century attitudes are looking better and better. If you happened to be amusing yourself at the Palladium in Manhattan, stoned, naturally, right to the eyeballs, and began muttering about "tight loops on the Tongariro" or something like that, people might naturally assume you'd gone beyond simple leather and nipple clips. Only the bold would inquire directly.

Do fishermen eat avocados? This is a question no one ever thinks to ask.

The distance from the barren lands north of Reykjavik to the Plaza at Century City is well over a hundred years. Several southern Californians who visit Century City frequently, and who see nothing terribly unusual about it, also visit Iceland to fish for salmon. They don't see anything very unusual about Iceland either.

I was invited once to equally remote country, where I was given to understand fly tying was done under suitable cover because there were so many fish. The invitation, I might add, meant only that there was space for me on the river; my hosts were not picking up the tab.

That little item was to run around $6,500 for the week.

"Gee, that's a lot," I said, with the same sense of helplessness a seven-year-old might feel looking at a full plate of string beans.

"The gillies fix a wonderful hot lunch every day."

"I got that free in public school."

Fishing is one of the least complicated endeavors available to human beings, yet of all the popular sports its devotees are the most likely to go off the deep end equipmentwise. I recently saw a new fishing vest with so many pockets inside and out that you'd be round if you put something in each one.

Fly fishermen appear to have the least resistance to the lure of gadgetry. Aside from the hundreds and hundreds of necessary rods, reels, lines, flies, vests, hats, boots and nets, there are other items you won't want to be without: a leather reel bag, textured rod grips (to pull your rod apart), a stripping basket (for those long casts), some no-knot eyelets (to fix line to leader), a gum-rubber leader straightener, fly-line conditioner, leader sinks, a wading staff, an assortment of fly boxes, leader packets, a casting glove, caulked sandals, wader patch, wader clasps, a net retractor, a hand-warmer, a knot-tyer, a micrometer, forceps (for removing hooks), scissors, pliers, a stream thermometer, a pocket magnifying glass, a hook hone, bug repellent, dry-fly spray, clippers, a streamside diary, an eyeglass snuggler, a mini-telescope (for identifying fly hatches), polarized glasses, a trout stomach pump, an insect inspection tray, larval forceps, a miniature battery-operated vacuum cleaner (to clean up after fly tying; batteries not included), a fly-tying vise, a bobbin, a whip finisher, a half hitcher, hackle pliers, tweezers, fly-tying materials (several pounds of these alone), a complete library of books; and, of course, the novelty items: belt buckles, tie clips, hat bands, ice buckets, cocktail glasses, prints and so forth. This is to say nothing of special vehicles, camping gear, boats and even possibly cabins and water leases.

The opening paragraph of Zane Grey's *Tales of Fishing Virgin Seas* goes like this: "A fisherman has many dreams, and from boyhood one of mine was to own a beautiful white ship with sails like wings, and to sail into tropic seas." He goes on to say that in 1924 he bought a "big three-masted schooner that, of the many vessels along the south shore of Nova Scotia, appeared to be the finest, and the most wonderful bargain. Her length was 190 feet over all, with beam of 35 feet, and she drew 11 feet, 6 inches of water. I changed the name *Marshall Foch* to that of *Fisherman,* and left my boatman, Captain Sid Boerstler, in charge to make the extensive changes we had planned. The work employed a large force of men for over three months."

Later he makes connections with his new ship in Panama.

I found my ship Fisherman *something to explore, and more satisfactory than I'd dared hope. Here at last was objective proof of my investment, and something worth possessing. The aftercabin had been built to extend over the forward hatch, and it contained eight staterooms and saloon. Galley and crew quarters were new. Below deck there was a combination saloon and dining room, four bathrooms, a darkroom for photography, tackle room, storerooms, a large refrigerator plant, half a dozen staterooms; and back of these the engine room, which had been Captain Sid's particular care and pride. It contained the two Fairbanks-Morse driving engines, and engine to generate electricity for the lights and fans, another for the compressed air that forced water over the ship, an emergency engine to use in case of accident to the electric generator, and automatic pumps and devices. The tanks were all built of steel, and fitted into the sides of the vessel. There were tanks for five thousand gallons of crude oil and one for cylinder oil; tanks for five thousand gallons of water and twenty-five hundred gallons of gasoline. In the forecastle was an engine to hoist sails and anchors; there were lathes, tool bench, forge, and carpenter shop.*

The Fisherman *carried three launches, one swung over the stern, lashed fast, the other two in cradles on the main deck between the main and mizzen masts. . . .*

For catching fish and battling the monsters of tropic seas we had every kind of tackle that money could buy and ingenuity devise.

Thereafter, Grey mounted a fishing expedition of truly imperialist proportions. And despite the readers' almost guaranteed distress in the face of Grey's uniformly prosaic prose, and his repeated use of such dialogue as " 'Darned if it isn't a tuna,' ejaculated R. C.," or, " 'Zowie!

61

Look at my line go,' exclaimed Romer. 'Now I'll have to wind all of it back,'" Zane Grey had fishing in his heart.

Everyone who has ever set pen to paper with regard to the topic of angling has either felt obliged, or else been asked by puzzled publishers, to explain why people fish. Never was it done with more style and grace than by the late Roderick Haig-Brown, a man whom many feel was the greatest angling writer in the English language. I still envy Haig-Brown's richness and clarity, his compassion, his attention to detail, and his perfect sense of pace. As hard as I may try, however, I cannot make Haig-Brown's experiences my own. There are as many reasons why and ways to fish as there are people who do it.

Of all the kinds of fishing, fly fishing, my preference, has been the one most often held under the magnifying glass and examined in terms so personalized as to obscure its inherent simplicity.

For instance, in Ray Bergman's *Trout,* a book which has been in print since 1938, and which has been described as "our Old Testament, the first and only book many anglers look to for guidance," there are ten pages of pictures of what are labeled "wet flies." By actual count this comes to exactly 4,068 separate fly patterns. "My God," the beginner tells himself with perfectly logical foresight, "if I buy two each in case I lose one on a branch there goes my new Pontiac."

Twenty-five years ago I had these same plates tacked on the wall of my room above the desk where I tied flies. Some of the names became familiar simply because they had a nice sound: the Black Prince, the Coachman, the Fish Hawk, Greenwell's Glory, Pale Evening Dun, Paramachene Belle, Whirling Blue Dun. Others, through some twist of fate such as the fact they were simply at eye level, became familiar too, though they were, as the saying goes, still Greek: Magalloway, Down Looker, Kiffe, Bostwick, Hoptacong, Brandreth, Mershon, Kinross, Fitzmaurice, Passadunk, Critchley Hackle. And so on.

It occurred to me early on that hardly one of the nearly five hundred vividly-pictured flies looked like something I'd want to go fishing with. I certainly never tied any of them at my vise even though they were laid out and completely titled in blueprint form before my very face. To this day, to the best of my knowledge, having fished with rather uncommon frequency for nearly four decades, I have never fished with one of them.

Yet fish have been caught on each of those strange concoctions or else they would not be there. And *Trout* also pictures another several dozen "bucktails and streamers," and perhaps a hundred and fifty kinds of "dry flies." In *Flies* by J. Edson Leonard, another popular book in print since 1950, 2,200 patterns are listed. With the exception of half a dozen not-too-close facsimiles, I've never fished with any of those, either. To apply a line of Miss Clavel's, from Bemelman's children's classic *Madeline,* "Something is not right!"

A friend bought a rather hefty and expensive coffee-table book entirely devoted to how trout eat floating bugs. There were many photographs and then more photographs, these overlaid with confusing diagrams concerning light refraction, a fish's angle of vision and some other things I became too impatient to understand.

"I don't get it," I said.

"No, of course you don't." My friend snapped back with one of those curious little half smiles the intelligentsia apply to hopeless cases. "That's because you oversimplify everything."

"I have more fun that way."

"If you took the time to sit down and study this book you'd see that the whole point of it is to simplify dry-fly fishing."

"Why don't I understand it, then? The only thing that makes sense to me is the page with the photo of the real bug and the fake one shown from beneath, the one with the caption that says neither is visible other than as a little shapeless blob. The picture proves it. I understand this picture fine. What I don't understand is the need for the other two-hundred pages."

"Why don't you take up bait fishing?"

"I have. It's fun."

"Figures."

"You take all this bullshit too seriously. Look at your fly-rod collection. You have all these Leonards, Paynes, Garrisons and what have you, worth enough to support a family for a year. I don't believe you can really tell the difference between them. In fact, I don't think nine out of ten so-called quality rod owners could tell the difference between their favorites and a fifteen-dollar dimestore job."

"You're joking."

"Not. I used to hang around with tournament fly casters. There

The sound of casting on Japanese radio.

aren't more than a handful of people who can do the job better than I can. Those guys, who were twice as good as I'll ever be, which is to say five times as good as you, used to laugh at rod snobs. That's where I got my sense of humor about it. So what it comes down to is what's called Pride of Ownership, which in nearly every case has far less to do with appreciating the craftsmanship than it does with firsthand acquaintanceship with the price sticker."

"Never mind."

The object of all this is a cold-blooded creature whose brain you could hide under a postage stamp. It is generally called a trout and comes in several varieties. Among these are the one native to Europe called the brown trout or sometimes the Loch Leven, described in books and magazines as being "the smartest." Writers of this genre speak often of "matching wits" with such and such an old lunker. One wonders whether a twenty-pound brown trout could solve the puzzle on *Wheel of Fortune.*

You inevitably come once again face-to-face with the imperialist point of view. Brown trout are most generally sought by elite anglers in elite surroundings. At the Angler's Club of New York they dispute the relative merits of the $400 Payne fly rod against the $700 Garrison. They refer to insects by Latin names, talk in hushed tones about rise forms, and when discussing water always use the possessive pronouns ours, his, mine or theirs. Among the membership, ladies, outdoor writers, those of Jewish descent, or persons of the colored persuasion are not to be found.

Several years ago a militant Puerto Rican group bombed an establishment adjacent to the Angler's Club, killing a number of persons. At the time, insiders admitted that the message left by the bombers indicated the real target was the Angler's Club itself, but the entrance to the Club was so inauspicious and obscure the bombers demolished the wrong target. Members of the Angler's Club had sufficient power to suppress the news.

If there is ever a revolution, trout and salmon fishermen will be the first to go up against the wall. Black bass and bream fishermen will either be in the audience or the firing squad.

With regard to the matter of conservation, a subject all fishermen at least claim to be interested in, the case is still wide open. The aforementioned Mr. Haig-Brown was not only convincing when he pleaded for its intelligent application, he was downright awe-inspiring. His sense of public justice could bring you to your feet.

The really tricky problems in resource management don't come up when you have more of the resource than people to use it. The hard part comes when millions of people compete for the same thing. Things have been this way in Europe for centuries, and are becoming this way in the United States. It is a difficult question, inextricably tied to politics: socialism versus capitalism. Do you let the people in or do you keep them out? Citizens with generally humanist beliefs on welfare with respect to medicine, housing, nourishment and human dignity often become raving fascists the moment natural resources become the topic. If I owned a large ranch in some remote area of the West and there was great hunting and fishing on the property, my inclination would be to post armed guards and otherwise land mine the boundaries. Of course, if I were a sportsman looking for someplace to hunt or fish that would make me extremely unhappy. As the owner, though, I would stand firmly behind my No Trespassing signs and become widely known as a prick.

Fifteen years ago the Stockman Bar in Livingston, Montana, looked about the way it probably did the day it opened. The owner then, a man of relentless energy and mirth, was not above whipping a revolver from beneath the bar and fanning it into the twenty-foot ceiling just to see what kind of tracks the cracking plaster would make. That the slugs sometimes went right on through into the apartment above—his own, thus empty—mattered not at all.

A mixed drink in the Stockman was bourbon and water (mostly bourbon) and cost fifty cents. It happened occasionally that a couple from out of town, usually overdressed, would come in and order a vodka tonic and a daiquiri. They got two bourbon and water.

One night a railroad worker was boasting about having caught some outrageous number of trout, about five times the limit on bullheads I think, and all from one hole in the river.

The bartender leaned over and eyed the man levelly.

"It's not going to be quite as much fun then next year, is it?"

In the Como Se Llama pickup truck at Deep Creek.

INTO THE COUNTRY,
OUT OF YOUR HEAD

At a dinner party one evening I met by chance a gentleman who had read several stories I wrote about fly fishing. He was drinking. I didn't chastise him for that; God knows I've done it myself. In any case, with each fresh scotch and soda he became ever more furiously animated, excusing himself by saying it just wasn't every day you got to talk to a kindred Brother of the Angle. His line of work precluded it; he was working on his second, or possibly it was his third, million.

Others at our table—for we were at a restaurant where your average diner rarely spoke above a whisper unless it was to congratulate the chef on his superb *quenelles*—were visibly aghast. My new acquaintance spilled his drink a good many times, usually during certain fits wherein he leapt from his chair upon recall of some particularly outstanding angling adventure from his own dim past. Once, spittle flew from his chin, hitting a dinner partner, as he insisted that a three-pound rainbow trout he caught was "the fattest son-of-a-bitch you ever saw."

He told one anecdote, though, which took me somewhat by surprise, since, his current tippling aside, he was a pretty straight-seeming fellow. He once went on a salmon-fishing expedition with some other businessmen. The trip, judging from his comments, was a very welcome relief from the transfer of stocks and bonds. It was a good trip, with enough fish to please everyone. Still, he had carried along an ace up his sleeve which he was reserving for just the right moment: in his billfold, sequestered among the credit cards, was a hit of clear windowpane. On the last day of fishing he washed it down with the morning's coffee. And although when pressed he could seem to remember little about it, it was a day, he said, he will never forget.

In thinking about it later, I determined my own interest in what it might be like to hit the stream loaded was lower than the Los Angeles River in August. It's not that the notion hasn't ever come to mind, but I never even drink beer when I'm fishing. And that is definitely not a mainstream abstention. This becomes curious only after you understand that when the papers describe someone as a user of dangerous drugs, that could be me. I don't want a life without them, any more than I want a life without good wine and fine meals. Drugs are to life what tires are to cars.

Well, what kind of tightassed attitude is that, you ask. Isn't the whole idea of going fishing to relax and have fun? Isn't drinking part of having fun? Don't you get the giggles after you've smoked a joint? A great rush out of a couple of white crosses? And doesn't a bit of acid to the brain send you reeling into other worlds of emotion and visual excitement?

You betchum, little beaver. All the same, here is the kind of tightassed attitude it is: for me fishing is not *that* kind of fun. It's much the same as painting and writing, both of which I think of as being fun. Fishing and hunting, painting and writing are all a mixture of childlike enthusiasm—fun if you will—and sharply focused energy. The successful combination of excited wonder and fierce effort produces a new sensation: satisfaction, perhaps the greatest thrill and most important goal in all our lives.

These things share something else as well. All are rich in history, and all are largely available to even the simplest and poorest among the great unwashed. The so-called blood sports, or any of the activities involving an outdoor chase of some sort, are only less universal than hunger and love, and at least as accessible as paper and pencil. There is some of it in everyone, if manifested only by an urge to pick flowers or watch birds.

One of the things that happens on drugs, and this is true in some degree of all of them with the possible exception of coffee, is that they make you think you are a good deal more clever than you are. This is not precisely an advantage when trying to compose something as complicated as a novel or a painting. Nor will it give much aid as you attempt to set a dry fly down near a rising brown trout, or stalk a whitetail buck through stands of willow and aspen along a riverbed.

When I first heard about LSD, in 1960 I believe it was, my informant assured me that this miracle substance would, among other things, enable me to observe the heartbeat of plants, and to see in a single grain of sand a complete diagram of the cosmos. At the time I thought he was a fool to believe such nonsense. Now, after having tried it thirty or forty times myself, I've revised that opinion. He was a complete imbecile. Oh, I've seen trees contort and elongate and quiver in some pretty peculiar ways, and more than once have had to lay awake far into the wee hours watching pinwheels on an otherwise dark ceiling. But I missed out on the Great New Truths. Maybe, as with séances, you have to believe it before you can see it.

Once, Tom McGuane and I were at the funeral of an old gent we had both known. The whole business was very somber, as such ceremonies normally are. Everyone's head was bowed as a sermon was given concerning the life beyond and how we are all God's servants, etc. Just as I was beginning to feel embarrassed that we were the only ones there out of a crowd of about two hundred not wearing suits, Tom leaned toward me and whispered, "See that stained-glass window?" I glanced up at it, having taken earlier notice of its distinct lack of Virgin Mary or saint. For all anyone knew, it was a huge sheet of multicolored shatterproof glass someone had fired a mortar at.

"Know where they got the idea for it?"

"No, where?" I whispered back.

"It's a cross section of a hemorrhoid."

I started laughing and couldn't stop, stern looks notwithstanding. And that's how it is with drugs.

Psychedelic drugs are an introspective experience. They make you think you can see different aspects of yourself. Because of that, I like to be around people, noise and chaos to see what new effect those things have on me. The only thing we ever know well in this life is ourselves, and drugs enable you to shift around in your skin, to take another seat for another point of view.

Interaction with others is a vital function of personality, and drugs twist that interaction like nothing else. I've never understood taking acid and then disappearing into the far fields for a little communing with nature. I don't want to be witty with a blade of grass, and I certainly can't imagine the blade of grass being witty with me. It reminds me of B. Kliban's wonderful cartoon showing people humiliating a salami.

The powerful effects of jealousy and envy cannot be discounted as moving forces. Jealousy and envy won't work for you if you are not completely yourself. I'm not suggesting, as Freud did, that money, fame, and having beautiful lovers are the main goals of the artist. One or more of those fits into anyone's scheme. But jealousy and envy are alone responsible for the superlative in any line of endeavor.

Needless to say, covetry is not the answer. No, to covet is to desire wrongly, at one remove. But if you see a man fly casting with breathtaking grace and control, you want to be able to do it also, to feel that feeling of achievement. You want to do it because it is so satisfying of itself, not because you want to downgrade the other man. Long-term satisfaction is a result of concentrated effort and plain hard work. I don't know; maybe some people are envious of really sloppy drunks and can't wait to get home and practice.

For my part, please don't walk within ten yards upwind of me with a joint while I'm sketching. Don't even whisper the word. And no alcohol with lunch either, no matter how appealing a glass of wine might be. Same while writing. And I refuse to have my shooting or fly casting confounded by foreign matter in the bloodstream. Don't want to see it, any of it. Not the smoothest Maui Madness all sticky and golden, nor the finest organic mescaline. Not even a rock—and this is admittedly a toughy—of pure cocaine the size of an extra-large grade AA Nulaid. Owsley could hold out a handful of good old blue and I'd turn on one heel as if he were a follower of Krishna panhandling for change in the Salt Lake City airport.

We express our insanity in different ways. Shrinks want you to be adjusted, happy, productive. Hell, anyone would buy a good list like that. One aspect of my own craziness is that I never work at night, and I don't use any of mother's little helpers during the day. Never, at any rate, if I'm fishing, hunting, writing or painting.

But back to Owsley, et al; come sundown I will happily relieve him of his stash. At gunpoint if need be. Another kind of fun is at hand. The skylight is dark, palette and brushes clean, the typewriter silent, the fly rods in their cases. This is not the hour of skill and invention, insight and observation; the hour to analyze and dissect, to compile and compare, to know the ecstasy of success, the despair of failure. It is the cocktail hour, time for overly elaborate meals and general silliness. In short, it is the hour of the horse's ass.

Drugs are a spectator sport. Not that people don't ever try to do things while ripped. On the contrary. In this age of marijuana, that spectacular duller of the senses, half the work force in the country survives the tedium of often pointless jobs by simply doing a doobie during coffee breaks. Needless to say, seldom are these folks concerned with decisiveness, aggressiveness, or just plain paying real close attention.

Fishing and hunting may be escapes for some people too. Who hasn't heard of someone getting out to the hunting camp and then never leaving the lodge or tent, preferring to just sit and get pickled, satisfied enough to be away from wife and job for a week. Escapism is not at all like moving toward an alternate reality.

It comes down to whether or not you want to be the driver or a passenger. I like to drive. And if I find myself in a position of having to go along just for the ride, a level of unbelievable tedium sets in. Tom Wolfe called the seventies the "Me" decade, and he was right. But I prefer not to buy it personally. I want some unfashionable goals and I want to understand something about what is Out There. Candy Staten sings, "I want to learn all I can about *meeee*." Good luck and goodbye.

The West Coast is the global epicenter of being laid back. I understand this better than most because I was born and raised there. Well, the whole generation that grew out of the flower children and political awareness is now sitting out there like a vast molasses slick, a stoned empire of indiscriminate consumers.

This has all been a very long-winded way of saying that if I were to go salmon fishing in Iceland, I would go out of my way to forget the chemicals. What would go along on the trip though, would be a spectrum of the best fishing tackle I could find, as complete a knowledge of the region, its people and its resources as I could possibly get from reading, and a firm desire to be as good an angler as ever set foot on those shores.

The author in the kitchen of the Bay Club, California's oldest duck club.

EATING AROUND

Three pairs of feet dangle in the tepid water near the Marquesas, twenty miles off Key West. If your eyes wandered up past those ankles, shins, knees and thighs, you would soon see three oversized asses parked on the gunwhale of an otherwise fast, sleek fishing skiff.

"Whose idea was it not to put the leftover dry-fried beef in the lunch?" Jim Harrison asks menacingly as he squints into the brutal June sun with his one good eye. He and Guy de la Valdene turn to look at me. "It was you, wasn't it? 'Oh, let's not put that in, it'll be too much out there in the heat. We have plenty with the Cuban sandwiches.' Well, let me tell you those sandwiches are a mere shadow of the ones we used to get. Christ, I mean they are *tiny*."

"It's the flit influence," I say, trying to cover up what was clearly a case of poor judgment. "You see all those guys running up and down Duval Street in bikinis and crew cuts? They don't want big, fat Cuban sandwiches. They want cold asparagus soup with a side of sprouts and Perrier to keep trim so the other homingtons will find them attractive in the evening down at the disco. Surely you can't hold me responsible for the Cuban-sandwich maker trying to please the town's major constituency."

"The dry-fried beef would have been nice to have," Guy says. "But we'll just go on in a little early and fix an hors d'oeuvre immediately. Now let's go try the North Face for a while."

The trim little skiff with its great burden moves slowly along the shore of the island. Guy is up on the platform in back, poling the boat along, Harrison is searching the horizon from the gunwhale, sipping a rum and coke, and I am standing on the foredeck, fly rod in hand, waiting for the approach of tarpon. Sometimes these periods of poling,

75

searching, and waiting can be excruciatingly long. It doesn't take much time for one's mind to drift to other topics, and one of the most persistent and interesting is always food.

For these purposes I'm glad we're not steelhead fishing in British Columbia. The fishing there is stupendous, but B.C. is no place to go for sophisticated cuisine, nor are the camps there suited to the do-it-yourselfer.

Now, your British Columbian loathes your French Canadian. In every way possible he considers the latter to be at best a horse's ass. Here people are in full reaction against "fancy food" (French), and in full support, though once removed, of clubfoot boiling and frying (English).

Half a dozen years ago, Michael Butler, Richard Brautigan, Guy and I found ourselves in Campbell River on Vancouver Island. With a gesture toward the water nearby, Brautigan offered to buy dinner. "Must be great seafood around here," he said.

We located what was described as "the best restaurant in town." No matter where you go there is one of these. There, we were favored with one of the most astonishing meals ever served. The details are lengthy, boring and disgusting, but the fresh-shrimp curry was a standout, a UFO based on Aunt Penny's white sauce, now somehow turned a dull gray. Curry flavor? Forget it. Mixed into this homemade quicksand was some rudely chopped celery, pimentos, and last and definitely least, a few tough canned shrimp, the largest of which would rest comfortably on a postage stamp. Entombed beneath it all was the rice, gelatinous and practically transparent.

"So much for fresh seafood," mumbled Brautigan.

It was in B.C. that I overhead one man advise another, "Don't eat breakfast in so-and-so's cafe. I ordered an omelette in there the other day and it was soft!" B.C. is one of the few places where they have puffy gray steaks that seem to have been simmered in water, fried eggs you can't slice with a razor blade and ravioli that are simply two plies of dough, with no filling, served in weak brown gravy. After eating for a while in western Canada you could compile an encyclopedia of bizarre and pointless foods, and have it illustrated by B. Kliban.

***

"What kind of hors d'oeuvre?" I ask without turning to address anyone in particular.

"What about fresh Szechuan noodles in sweet chili paste?"

"We ate all the noodles."

"We could get some stone-crab claws."

"Don't bore us. That's for a ladies bridge club luncheon."

"Then you think of something."

"How about crispy pork dumplings? Or we could steam them. Better yet would be a bastardized mu shu pork where we double the ginger and garlic, add some chilis, and shoot some hot sesame oil in with the green onion and hoisin."

"That sounds good. Now, what can we have for dinner?"

"How about fresh yellowtail?"

"Fixed how?"

"Remember when we did it steamed over those veg . . . oh, shit!"

"What?"

"Son-of-a-bitch went right under the boat. Ninety, maybe a hundred pounds."

"Hmmm."

"Your turn to fish, Jim."

"You know," Jim says, gesturing with his cigarette, "we didn't come thousands of miles to go fishing just to have you not pay any attention and let all the fish swim under the boat. Get it? You have to look at the water or there's no point to any of this. Can't you think of anything except filling your big fat stomach?"

"I don't know, but there's a school of rollers heading our way and your fly line is all tangled around your feet."

"What! Jesus!"

"Just kidding. Wanted to see if you were paying attention after coming all these thousands of miles."

Guy's always calm voice interrupts. "Listen, Bubbleass and Needledick, we actually do have a string of fish coming in at about ten o'clock."

Harrison begins frantically pawing at the fly line. "C'mon now," he pleads hysterically. "Watch my line so it doesn't get hung up."

He makes his false casts with that sense of terror and urgency associated with fly fishing for tarpon, releasing the line only to have the headwind push it back into an unruly pile. Before he can recover, the

77

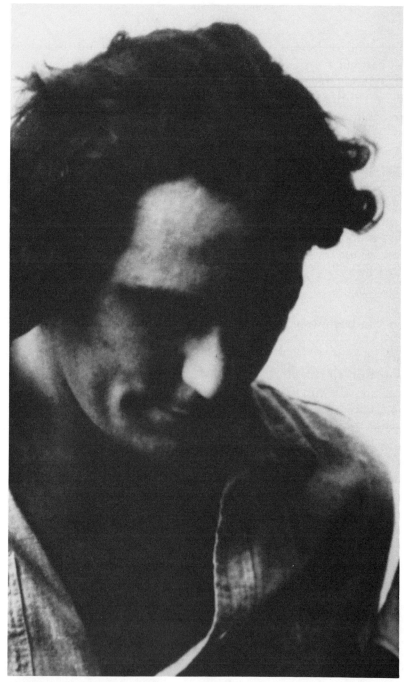

Guy de la Valdene.

tarpon have seen the boat and spook away, out of sight.

"Goddamn it." Jim moans with an absolutely sincere air of dejection.

The biggest difference between tarpon fishing with Jim and Guy in Key West during May, and bird hunting with them at Jim's home in Michigan during October (aside from the fact birds fly and fish swim, ha ha), is that while we never kill the tarpon, we most assuredly do kill the birds. We kill them not because we like to, but because you can't really prepare them for the table while they are still flying around.

The best part of Jim's house is the basement where the wine is. What could be finer than passing the time strolling among the bottles? The more superlative vintages are reserved for the more exotic meals, the ones to which guests are strictly excluded.

One of the most exquisite, if not the most exquisite meal of the entire fall, is one which Guy makes with woodcock: *salmis de bécasses à l'ancienne Christian Bourillot.* Guy not only makes the dish, he usually shoots the woodcock too, because Harrison misses them regularly, and as for myself, I may as well stay home trying to kill flies by slow pitching a softball at them.

The preparation of the salmis of woodcock involves not only sensitivity, but real knowledge of French cuisine. Of course, the woodcock will have been hung, undrawn and unplucked, for at least several days to develop and heighten their unique wild flavor. Roasting of the birds is done in a very hot oven for perhaps seven or eight minutes so the meat remains rare.

The sauce, which is enormously important, is made by browning the chopped carcasses in a *mirepoix* with butter, then flaming them with cognac, adding wine, and then combining the reduced liquid with a demi-glace. This is finally strained over the pieces of bird as they rest on croutons fried in butter and spread with intestines and foie gras. The heads are used as a garnish, the tiny brain considered a delicacy. When we are in line for this princely meal, the part of the cellar we look hardest at contains the old Margaux, Rothschilds, or Echézeaux.

"Let's look at the face of Ballast Key on our way in."

"I'll pole," I offer, "and Guy can fish for a change."

"You're not going to like it," Guy says with a twisted smile. "It's

79

a hard bottom, it's deep and the swells from the Atlantic make it a real bitch just to balance on the platform let alone pole."

"Let Mr. Hotshot give it a try."

"Listen, I've poled here before. It's not that big of a deal."

Standing on the platform is a little like walking a tightrope, not that I've ever walked one or ever will. But your feet and legs have to learn not to fight it, so you're not continually struggling for balance. Poling with the eighteen-foot fiberglass pole is not easy under the best of circumstances, and Guy was dead right when he described this spot.

I can't help but notice that my great weight is doing nothing to improve my poling technique and I wonder if there isn't a chance of obtaining some appreciable weight loss by devoting myself entirely to *nouvelle cuisine*. This passes through my mind only moments before the pole slips off the rocky bottom on a particularly difficult stroke, sending me straight into the ocean.

"Oh, for Christ's sake." Harrison rolls his eyes skyward, letting his arms hang exaggeratedly low at his sides.

"I think big boy needs a drink and some nourishment after all that poling."

"Yeah. And all that swimming."

A person who likes to eat and drink can really pull the plug in San Francisco. It has everything from the world's best hamburgers (at Clown Alley on Columbus), to the world's most esoteric and exotic foods (from, as they say, the four corners of the earth). And, as San Francisco is a very small city, your choice for the evening is never more than minutes away.

As big fans of the cooking of the Far East, where Marco Polo went to learn how to make spaghetti, Jim, Guy and I more often than not find ourselves in Chinatown, or close to it. Typically, we might go to the Great Eastern on Jackson Street, a place Brautigan showed us some years ago.

There, we might order sizzling rice soup, Mongolian lamb, asparagus beef, clams in black-bean sauce, snow peas with pork, almond pressed duck, fried prawns with plum sauce, sesame chicken, and usually three or four other vegetables or fish dishes depending on the season. We are often ridiculed by the otherwise dispassionate waiters.

Or we might try the Szechuan on Polk Street, where the Peking duck is as good as it gets. Given the time we would also hurt ourselves at Thai, Indonesian, Vietnamese, Indian, Japanese, and Hunan restaurants, too.

For Italian food, day in and day out you can't beat Vanessi's, although Modesto Lanzone's is awfully good, as is La Pergola. Unfortunately, the image of Italian food has been distorted through the influence of many heavy-handed restaurants that persist in serving murdered pasta with nasty, heavy, simmered-to-death tomato sauce. If Grandma simmered her special spaghetti sauce all day, it was because she was an uninformed geek who had watched one too many Ragu commercials on the tube.

Italian cuisine is among the most diverse and brilliant in the world, but it is totally dependent upon fresh ingredients, spontaneous preparation, and cooks who are imaginative, vigorous, and possess a generous and compassionate spirit. Italian dishes, like Mexican dishes, are seldom done well outside the regions of their origin.

For seafood, one is well advised to steer clear of the tourist ninnyism of Fisherman's Wharf, and stick to someplace like Tadich's or Scott's on Lombard. Or else order dishes made with fresh crab or salmon or whatever at good French, Italian, Chinese or continental places like Jack's or Ernie's.

My favorite French restaurant in the city is Le Castel out on Sacramento Street. It is arguably the best restaurant in San Francisco, except that it seems pointless to make that kind of statement because there are so many other wonderful places. When Sam Lawrence, the publisher, was in town, I took him over there knowing he'd love it. Sam devotes the same attention to getting good food and wine as another man might to freeing his foreskin from a hastily raised zipper. You need a wallet full of credit cards to eat there—you probably wouldn't want to carry that much cash around the streets—but it's well worth it. I got lucky on this particular night; Sam outgrappled me.

I think we had a lobster bisque and an exquisite appetizer of quail *en croûte*. The entrées were boned squab with chanterelles and green peppercorns in a honey-vinegar sauce, and an almost surreal pressed duck with pink peppercorns that was so beautifully presented I could barely stand to touch it with my fumbling knife and fork. We naturally availed ourselves of the very pleasant wine list.

81

My discovery of Le Castel was a black day for my otherwise long-suffering banker, who has since checked into an intensive care ward with high blood pressure and terminal ulcers. He wanted to know why I couldn't do something I could afford, like jump into an ice-cold river and float downstream for four or five miles.

I can't help myself. Think of it: salmon mousse awash in a *beurre blanc* in which sea urchins were puréed, then sautéed and garnished with a crayfish, or breast of pheasant in black-currant sauce, or saddle of lamb with fresh tarragon served with veal- and lamb-kidney mousse, or scallop and salmon pâté with lobster sauce, or rouget or lotte or barbue—all magnificently prepared—and a perfectly stunning array of desserts, all served by a battalion of well-informed, charming and energetic waiters.

Our arrival back at the dock is always unheralded. The dockmaster and other nautical types who never seem to do anything but watch the boats come and go never see us unload any fish although we go out every day. One of them asked about this once and our answer—that we didn't like to see the tarpon get too tired—seemed to alert the good old boys that there was something half a bubble off level about the three fatsos. Now they sort of look the other way when we tie up.

Even though we are now tired, sunburned, hot and irritable, we must make some stops on the way home. First is the Overseas Market, a vegetable store where we've been shopping for years. They have ginger root and shallots, leeks, pea pods, new potatoes, avocados, good fruit, and all the other assorted vegetables we ever need to prepare the overly large, overly elaborate, overly rich meals with which we daily shorten our lives.

The next stop is essential if we expect to remain alcoholics: Big Daddy's Liquors. There we are sure to stock up on Stolichnaya, Barbancourt or Mount Gay rum, scotch and whatever wine we can find, though getting anything very good is always a problem in Key West.

We then go to Faustos, where, among other things, Harrison insists we buy the ingredients for a *puttanesca* sauce—mainly tomatoes, garlic, olives and anchovies—"In case we get hungry at four in the morning just before turning in."

Last stop is the fish market on Duval near the adult bookstore, a most inappropriately named establishment.

"The yellowtail looks good, and the guy says it's fresh."

"Okay. And I'm getting some stone-crab claws no matter what you think."

"Let's go look at the dildos and stuff."

"My God, look at the size of the double-ender!"

"Yeah, well look at this magazine, *Ass Master's Special*. Or here's *Girls Who Like Big Cocks*."

"Put that down. There's no point in you looking at that."

"Let's buy a couple of poppers and then go over to the Havana Docks and watch the hippies clap when the sun sets."

I never would have guessed that shooting was the national sport of France until I went there. From about September through the end of the year, every single man, woman and child in the entire country discharges a firearm at least once at something that walks or flies. In conversation about it, your French upland bird hunter is extremely intense and colorfully descriptive. He uses the term *paff* to indicate his gunshot, and the term *plaff* to indicate the sound of his bird hitting the ground. *Paff! Paff! Plaff.* Like that.

A couple of seasons ago I was there with Guy, Michel Jeuffrain, Jimmy Buffett and Bob Dattila, ostensibly to hunt pheasants, pigeons, partridges and ducks. We shot the pigeons from high towers constructed in the woods, the pheasant and partridge were driven to us by beaters, and the ducks were somehow just there.

At the beginning of our visit, we stayed at a huge, marvelous, renovated mill, which rivaled the magnificent 14th-century château on the same property. The house was so large we found ourselves consistently unable to locate either each other's rooms or our own. We constantly opened wrong doors only to discover yet another huge room hung with paintings, with yet another old couple seated in front of yet another Sony color television set.

Anyway, the duck hunt was something of an afterthought, because our host felt the pigeons appeared that morning in insufficient numbers. We were directed to station ourselves around the château. This seemed deeply odd, so I asked Michel where in the hell they thought the ducks were going to come from.

"Do not worry monsieur, they will arrive."

And arrive they did, about ten minutes after our host had rousted

Jim Harrison about to release a small tarpon.

them off his lake. Wings set, the fifty or so mallards came dropping back in to home base. Only thirty-eight of them made it.

Guy and I fixed the birds that evening and it was a wonderful treat for me to cook in this provincial kitchen with its large pantry filled with fresh herbs and garden vegetables. We ate all the ducks with a great French Bordeaux, and ended up covered with grease, drunk, and totally silly.

One might convincingly argue that Parisians live for food, love and fashion, not necessarily in that order. In the morning, over croissants and coffee with their lovers, they discuss lunch, and at lunch they argue about dinner, and at dinner they are thinking of bed. They dress appropriately for all four.

The eating seemed endless to us, a dirty job as it were. But someone had to do it. We had tiny red and gray shrimp and five kinds of oysters at La Coupole one day, a classic veal roast at Lipp the next, and an elegant little meal at Castel's the day after that.

One night we ate at Caspia, the caviar dealers, in a kind of upstairs Russian Tea Room. We opened a kilo of the finest gray caviar in the world, fresh from the Caspian Sea, the tiny, perfect eggs languishing sensually in their unique container. We had a superb vodka, commercially unavailable outside of Russia, which our host provided. After the caviar was gone, we had Scottish smoked salmon with blintzes, and to finish, a beautifully clear borscht. You couldn't have a simpler or more regal meal.

Perhaps the single most extraordinary meal we had was at the restaurant Faugeron. When we entered it was very quiet, all the other customers were sheiks, and there were more waiters than patrons, all clues as to what these little snacks were going to set us back.

They didn't have the ragoût of truffles that night, a dish Guy had assured me was one of the most remarkable on the face of the earth. They did, however, have the saddle of hare, which, beyond any shadow of a doubt, is the single most delightful bit of food I've ever tasted.

When we departed Paris, I had gained about twenty pounds, my face was continually flushed and simply breathing was difficult. One afternoon at the Louvre I nearly passed out after eating a gargantuan lunch with Buffett and Dattila somewhere along the Seine. I thought for sure it was the big moment, but it wasn't.

The Havana Docks bar is a very nice place to have some drinks.

We go there just about every evening at around sundown to have a few. Tonight we've had about six and they were very large, so, predictably enough, we are now drunk. Following in the great tradition of the people of every civilization since the beginning of recorded history, we are absolutely shitfaced.

"Jim," I say, "about a month ago in San Francisco I was listening to the radio and on the news they said the highway patrol reported that an unidentified man had fallen out of his car on the Golden Gate Bridge. They said it happened about six o'clock in the morning when he was on the way home from a birthday party and he stood up through the open sun roof to take off his shirt. You know why he fell out of his car? I'll tell you why. It was because that fellow had had too much to drink."

"Ungh." Harrison's eye stares off to one side at a potted palm. "What are you telling me? That we should never go to birthday parties or wear shirts?"

"I don't know, but I'm just very fond of picturing that driverless car gradually coming to a stop about three hundred yards away from its former operator. I also think we should shitcan our original plans for dinner and just walk across the street to Chez Emile, go up and sit on the balcony and order ourselves some bottles of Montrachet and a roast duck."

Swiveling efficiently off his bar stool, Guy says softly, "You got it."

In Honolulu, a tourist guide called "This Week in Oahu" advertises a restaurant called Bagwell's. A photograph of the handsome sommelier is accompanied by the slogan, "The Bagwell's Evening . . . more than an evening, it is an event." Someone told me that dinner for three there had run them around eight hundred dollars. For reasons not known to God or my mom, this did not seem to deter me. It was, in fact, more like waving a red flag in front of a bull. One can drink drinks that look like lawn furniture, and eat barbequed ribs or pizzas that taste like old socks and used kleenex respectively for only so long. Bagwell's it was, then.

Hawaii is a strange place. There's the Don Ho program, some exquisite mountains, jungles, and a few lonely beaches. Between that there is this rather enormous lumpen mystery, not precisely à la Gertrude Stein's appraisal of Oakland (there is no *there* there), but close. The Japanese evidently control things economically and politically, while the native Hawaiians struggle to maintain the very threadbare cloth of social history so unique to these islands. Other than that, there exists a great melting pot of people from the Pacific Rim, including Orientals of every persuasion, Filipinos and Samoans, the latter a group of exceptionally large individuals whose main occupation seems to be punching non-Samoans in the nose.

Several years ago when Mick Jagger learned his group was to play in the islands, he remarked, "Hawaii? I don't want to go to Hawaii. What is there to fuckin' buy in Hawaii?"

For one thing, he could have bought Peter Fonda's yacht *Tatooch,* moored off Oahu, and learned firsthand why owning an enormous oceangoing sailboat has been described as being similar to standing in an ice-cold shower tearing up hundred dollar bills.

Before going to Bagwell's I was quite peckish, so it seemed sensible to eat a couple of sweet Chinese sausages, washed down with two vodka tonics. After that, I walked over to the Hyatt Regency where I was to meet my date. There we had two gigantic Bombay-gin martinis at a bar called Trappers. At the restaurant itself we started with oysters (very small and fresh), shrimp bisque (tasty), terrine of veal sweetbreads (excellent), pork and veal pâté (okay), papaya, avocado, shrimp and watercress vinaigrette (perfect), and a bottle of Montrachet (just right!). After that it was *tournedos Rossini* (only about a C+), veal chop with truffles (much better), potatoes au gratin and french green beans (ho hum), and a bottle of Heitz Martha's Vineyard Cabernet (yes!). To finish, there were several snifters of a very good Napoleon cognac (what could be finer?), and I skated out of there for just a shade above two-fifty, completely dizzy, stuffed, and six pounds heavier.

The night being young, illegal drugs came immediately to mind, but none could be located. Instead, I cleverly chopped up half a dozen diet pills and snorted the whole mess. Then it was off to a very interesting nightclub where, with plenty of cocktails, we watched beautiful women perform feats of imagination and daring with their private parts. For instance, one girl stacked quarters on top of a beer bottle, then had intercourse with the pile of quarters and the beer bottle, removed the bottle, and then proceeded to hand out quarters to patrons in any denomination she wished. Another girl played a pretty good flute using her you know what. She also wrote little cards to people while she was sitting on a swing holding the pen in the same place. My handwriting isn't nearly that good. After that she swung with abandon out toward the audience, a bright-green fluorescent dildo held firmly between her legs until, at the height of her forward trajectory, she fired it end over end across the club. The first one hit a bewildered Samoan in the chest. I caught mine and took it home.

The last act was performed by a vivacious and beautiful lady named Kim. She first appeared onstage in an outrageous feathered costume, which she soon removed. At the end of her dance, she squeezed out a hardboiled egg which rolled onto the stage. She then peeled it, rinsed it with Heinekens and put it back. Thus loaded, she fired this and subsequent eggs great distances and with uncanny accuracy. Later, she instructed me to open my mouth, which I did, and she whipped out a line drive that scored a bull's eye.

I liked the acts so well I insisted we stay for the second show (which gave us a chance to have a few more cocktails). For some unknown reason, I began compulsively eating the popcorn which was on our table. Three boxes of popcorn and about ten straight vodkas later the show was over and it was time to go.

Did we go home? No. Instead we decided to play some Space Invaders—right after having a few more mashed up diet pills which would be sure to sharpen the old eye. If you don't know what Space Invaders is, I'm not going to tell you. It's just the most important thing in Hawaii, that's all.

Across from the Space Invader game room was a cowboy bar where you could repair for a little refreshment, something I did frequently since my firing rocket always got blown up right away. At the time, there was the distinct feeling we hadn't yet had enough to drink.

About four in the morning I had a beer, some salami and Japanese crackers, two Alka Seltzers (in the beer), a tranquilizer, a codeine tablet and a Bufferin. Before passing out I recall being pleased to have survived the Bagwell's Evening, although I'm sure this is not precisely what the tourist guides had in mind.

It has gotten late. After finishing dinner at about midnight, we felt the need for a nightcap at the Full Moon Saloon, and of course it took a couple of hours to get that done. Now we are standing around the kitchen of our house drinking a beer at three-thirty, wondering if we should make ourselves a little pasta. In a rare display of intelligence, Guy goes to bed. Jim and I open the refrigerator and stare into it dumbly as if waiting for a recorded message to tell us what to do next.

With a certain air of resignation we close the door knowing that 1) we're too drunk to make it right, and 2) we're too tired to eat it if we did.

In my room, the house very quiet now, I find myself extremely pleased that I didn't drive to the Boca Chica bar to shoot pool until seven in the morning. As Harrison said in a poem he once gave me, what keeps you alive as an artist is chance, mobility and sleeplessness. He's right of course, but I think I've done my job for the day, and the low-rent hustlers at the bar will have to find another boob to trick money out of this morning. My room has gotten very dark.

DARK WATERS

Phil Wood shad fishing on the Yuba River.

SHAD: RATS!

Round de Bend He Go

In spite of a badly deteriorated memory, I can recall the first fish I ever caught on a fly very clearly. It was a shad. The month was May, the year was—let's call it 1953.

There is no faith quite like blind faith. I hadn't the remotest notion what I was doing when that fish intercepted its fate. Not that there was any mortality involved; at the time, if you wished to remain on morally stable ground, you released all your shad. But even a blind hog finds an acorn once in a while.

I don't want to suggest there were no clues at all; that would be completely misleading. I was fishing that day, a Saturday, on the Russian River at a pool called Summer Home Park. This hole was already known along the river as a good place for shad fishing. Shad had been caught there since the last years of the war.

Carl Ludeman, who developed the basic shad fly which today bears his name, had a cabin at Summer Home Park. He fished the pool regularly. So did Jules Cuenin, a fine angler who for years did the outdoor column for the *San Francisco Examiner*. Once he wrote, ". . . the lower end of the Summer Home Park hole is good for shad in the evening just before dark. Make a long cast and as it swings release some line so the fly goes deep into the pool. The shad hit at the end of the swing."

You could only get to the pool during spring months by approaching it from the other side. You had to drive to Hilton, the next pool downstream, then walk up. The summer foot bridge was never put up until Memorial Day at the earliest. Hilton had a certain reputation as a shad hole, so that morning I tried it first but without luck.

Arriving later at the head of Summer Home beach, I was surprised and excited to see shad scales on the ground. Someone had recently landed a shad there. The fish have very large scales which are easily disturbed when you beach them. I felt a surge of confidence. The night before I had seen shad knifing around the surface of the pool, something they do as part of their spawning behavior.

I began casting and working down through the riffle. At one point I encountered the inevitable back eddy, which caused line nearest the rod to swing upstream while the fly moved down, eventually to rest in the dividing line between opposing currents. This was hardly ideal, but in my complete naiveté I went on with it and this is exactly where the hog found his nut. Heart pounding like a drum, my virginity was gone like flecks of foam around a bend in the stream.

From that moment on I was obliged to view shad with a special fondness. And for the next ten years I never failed to put in a reasonably vigorous season, not only on the Russian River, but on streams in the Sacramento Valley as well.

Steelhead fishermen first discovered what a treat catching shad could be; whether by accident or design doesn't matter. Steelhead season is over in March. Shad fishing—which involves long casts and a fish with enough weight to be interesting—can be extended clear into July.

Early on, shad were wholly enigmatic to western fishermen. Shad are distinctly saltwater fish in appearance, resembling both the tarpon and herring to whom they are closely related; they appear out of place when found in the same water as salmon and steelhead. In a stream fifty or a hundred miles from the coast, you think for a moment there's been some mistake. Shad are not a native fish of the West Coast. Like striped bass, they were brought from the east and planted in the San Francisco Bay delta. From there they extended their range, according to most sources, from San Diego to Alaska. I have no idea what rivers they might enter south of the Russian. They are not common in Alaska, either, although runs are reported from the Kodiak Island region and as far west as Asia.

When the adults run into rivers to spawn they are totally non-competitive for food or spawning territory with any other species. Their normal food, which is said to be plankton, is not present and so, like many other anadromous species, they simply cease feeding during the spawning journey. Shad are broadcast spawners like striped bass; this task is generally done at night, near the surface, and most often in relatively slow-moving water. Watching the water at night is a very handy way of determining if there are shad present, and if so how many.

In common with many other migratory fish, shad strike readily at a variety of lures and have been caught on every imaginable type of bait. However, they seem most fatally attracted to something that glitters and shines.

The Russian River, where shad fishing in the West began, is never a clear stream. It is naturally slow moving and silty, winding out of the wine country. During fall months just before the rains and after the hordes of summer swimmers have gone home, visibility reaches a peak of six or seven feet. In the springtime the Russian runs high, and the best you ever get is a milky green, akin to the appearance of glacial rivers.

In the years before the great runs of the Sacramento were fully appreciated, the Russian was the main river for shad fishing. Because it hid its runs of fish beneath turbid flows, few people knew much about how shad behaved. This gave rise to any number of absurd theories and suppositions.

The earliest of these was the myth of the glass bead. Shad most certainly strike well at glass beads, but they strike just as well at diamond rings, pop tops and bare silver hooks. To this day some staunchly believe the beads are magic, going so far as to carry a supply of them in various shades. Some fly fishermen do the same with flies. I don't know. A change from silver and orange to silver and blue definitely gets a rise out of steelhead or salmon that have been watching the orange go by for awhile. The main thing the beads did, certainly important in heavy water, was to get the lure, or fly if you will, deeper. During the 1940's the only available line was silk, which didn't sink very fast. Glass beads go down like sinkers.

The Ludeman shad fly has a red tail, silver body, white hackle, and red chenille head. When fluorescent colors came in, some people used these colors in the chenille. Carl used to carry one other fly he would sometimes switch to if he felt the shad were ignoring his standard pattern. This alternate fly had a gold body, brown hackle, and brown chenille. I think he called it a brown cow. In all the years I've fished for shad, the basic pattern tied in sizes four down through twelve has done the job nicely. The exception happens during very low water years, or very late in the season. At these times any number of buggy-looking trout flies often work better.

In common with steelhead, not all shad die after spawning; in fact, the majority do not. The situation may vary from river to river but a twenty-percent mortality rate is a reasonable estimate. Again, as with steelhead, after spawning the spent fish work their way slowly downstream, gathering strength. At this time they begin to seek food deliberately. They don't find much, especially in the case of shad where the schools contain hundreds of fish, but when something edible comes within range, it is eagerly eaten. When shad are from four to seven months old, or from three to six inches, they surface feed steadily on various hatching insects. During what trout fishermen call a spinner fall on a late summer evening, thousands of shad fry can be seen dimpling up for the inert, drifting flies.

It should not therefore be entirely surprising that given the right conditions, shad respond to nymphs and even dry flies. With regard to the latter, I've never had a shad take a free-floating dry; it must be skated or moved. This is not a negative necessity. I rarely fish a free-floating dry for trout, or an upstream dry either for that matter. The takes are more lively and aggressive on the moving fly.

When fishermen started going over to the Valley streams—the Sacramento, American, Feather and Yuba rivers—they faced a revelation. To someone who had known only the Russian River, the numbers of shad in these other rivers was nearly incomprehensible. A good day on the Russian might be a dozen fish, a great day, twenty-five or thirty. A good day in the Valley was at least fifty and if you had the interest and the stamina you could triple that figure.

Most advances in knowledge happen when the fishing is very good. I begin to experiment with this or that because I actually tire of the repetition which occurs with one method. I always knew if something didn't work when I fished the Valley rivers I could come back to what would, and thus always be able to bail myself out of what ordinarily would be frustrating circumstances.

Fishing the Yuba for instance, I might walk away from masses of fish just to see if some other very unlikely water was any good. And more than one angler found himself changing flies to something seemingly preposterous just to find out what would happen.

Once on the Feather River when fishing was awfully good, we started reducing the size of our flies until they were down as small as twenty-two. The water was very clear, but moving right along. Strikes were plentiful, proving that shad are extraordinarily keen-eyed, something I'd never have known if I was still fishing the Russian. Later, having that knowledge learned on the Feather in mind, we caught shad on the Russian when it was low and clear by using tiny flies.

Shad fishermen experience what they call "bumps." This is not a skin disease. When the line is swinging, shad often tap the fly and this is telegraphed up the line. Usually there is not one tap, but two or three or four. We used to think it was a shad following the fly. The clear water of the Valley streams revealed the truth: four bumps were four different fish. As the fly passed by a group of shad, each of the four— or five, or three, or two—bumped it without breaking rank, thus maintaining the specific hierarchy and arrangement of the school. Sometimes one of these fish was hooked. More often though, a hooked shad was one that broke a bit away from the ranks and hit with true determination.

At first we turned all our shad back, partly because we imagined ourselves to be sporting types, partly because it was a very clean solution to the problem of what to do with them, and partly because they just didn't look or smell right. Their nickname was Halitosis Herring. We did all this in the face of the hard fact that so-called planked shad was considered a gourmet's treat in eastern restaurants, and shad roe commanded a stiff price everywhere. I killed a few females in deference to my father's pleading but personally found the sauteed results unpleasing. But then, teenagers are seldom much interested in the esoteric.

Those who had kept some shad and cooked them were universal in their denouncement of the fish as an edible commodity. The reason always turned out to be the million or so bones that crisscross the flesh. There were, though, quasi-country types who saw fields and streams as supermarkets without checkstands. These fellows would keep a foul-hooked flounder, planning to fry it with zucchini for lunch. Such fishermen did two things with shad: smoked them, or pressure-cooked them long enough to disintegrate the bones. The former was not half bad. The latter. . . well, it would have been simpler and cheaper just to have bought oatmeal in the first place.

I read somewhere that to prepare a shad for the dish known as planked shad, essentially a boneless filet with skin attached, a professional had to work for fifteen to twenty minutes on one fish. That meant a klutz like me was looking at an hour and fifteen minutes. Once, in zoology class, one of the students complained to the teacher that a certain frog artery wasn't where it was supposed to be. The teacher, a pretty mellow old gent, smiled and said, "The frog is always right." I liked that. So when it came down to cases, I killed a shad and took it home determined to dissect it completely in the interest of firsthand information.

The talk of bones was not exaggerated. These things were a nightmare. Still, as with everything in nature, you could find a pattern. As to the odor, I concluded it was in the skin, as it is with most fish, so I determined to find a way to make something to eat out of the shad that was both skinless and boneless.

The system I finally settled on might seem a bit on the wasteful side to some, but it's the best I can do. Start by filleting a large shad into two halves. Females are best because they are the biggest and also because of the roe they provide. This roe is absolutely exquisite when fresh, in spite of what teenagers think. Laying them skin down, find the bone structure with your fingertips, and using a very sharp, small knife, trim boneless pieces of meat out of this slab.

The meat itself is easily on a par with pompano. It's moist and succulent, very pale, and almost white after cooking. Once you have the boneless strips you're ready for a variety of recipes from simple sautéing with wine, garlic, lemon and butter, to tempura, to any of a dozen dishes eaten with reduced hollandaise-type sauces. The meat is so exquisitely delicate you must force yourself not to overcook it. In fact, it's perfect as sashimi. Care must be taken, however, to see that the shad is handled properly and put on ice immediately after it is caught. It should be eaten very shortly thereafter.

If you think I'm now going to close by suggesting a person's first fly-caught fish stands on anywhere near equal footing with his or her first lover, you're only half right. I can be corny but not that corny. My first lover changed my life a good deal more than my first fish on a fly. Leave it at that.

But as I said at the beginning, I maintain a special fondness for shad and shad fishing, and that will never change. In the early days we thought of them as being tailored to the whims and hopes of fly fishermen because they took so well and filled the rivers during spring when it is appropriate to be full of hope.

Some things are missing from shad fishing which are essential elements otherwise. Shad are more or less all the same size, so there is little or no trophy angle. And fly selection, so much a part of trout fishing, is insignificant here. Even with regard to the kitchen, most people remain confused or indifferent.

Shad fishing at its best implies a lack of motives, except the seeking of simple pleasure. I have personal reasons for adoring the whole business as I do, reasons merely touched upon here. I'm indebted to the smelly things I guess, but when I think it through I wonder if it really was a favor.

Moe.

THE WORLD'S GREATEST TROUT STREAM

Some of you may wonder how I can have the brass to follow such a story title with the story itself. Everything I tell you herein will be the absolute truth. Hard as you may search, however, you will find no real clues as to the locale of this extraordinary water. The reason, simply enough, is that this may be the only pristine place left on Earth. A very small handful of people have ever seen it during recorded history. It is as fragile as a butter cookie in the hands of Jabba the Hut. Assuming a certain degree of guile and efficiency, two common traits abundant in the character of successful poachers, one unscrupulous meat packer could kill most of the trout in this waterway in one day. Given three, not a fish would be left alive.

So, I think you can see why I will not divulge the county, state, country, continent or even hemisphere of this perfect river. The names of my companions will obviously be fictitious and you will find neither flora nor fauna correctly named. Forget about wondering where this stream is, and consider instead what will be lost when this river is discovered and the Trout Unlimited gang march in. Think about Janet Leigh before and after her shower in *Psycho*.

An interesting side note to this story is that I dreamed of fishing a river like this when I was twelve or thirteen years old. Where I grew up, in Marin County, California, we had plenty of good fishing and hunting. I can hardly go back there today because I'm not a masochist. Viewing corpses just isn't my idea of a good time. But that's another story.

Anyway, up on the north slope of Mt. Tamalpais, flowing into Alpine Lake, is a beautiful stream called Cascade Creek. My friend Kelly

Dunigan located it on his map, and we rode our bikes to the dam one Saturday, and then walked up to the creek.

Cascade Creek is made up mostly of waterfalls too steep for fish to negotiate up or down, so obviously someone must have planted a few little trout in it once. It is not good fishing. But you have to remember that there is really no trout fishing per se on the California coast. The native fish are the seagoing rainbow trout known as steelhead. Young steelhead from seven to twelve inches can be caught in all the creeks and rivers, but even at that age, Kelly and I knew they were best released so they could go to the ocean and come back as seven to twelve pounders.

These little fish in Cascade Creek were going nowhere, however, unless they wanted to go over a few fifty-foot falls down into Alpine Lake. So Kelly and I told each other we were trout fishing.

The only pool I remember was the one on which my fantasy was based. We had walked along the steep, fern-lined trail for some distance, then climbed up a steep, rocky face. At the top we peered over the lip and looked across an almost magical pool right at eye level. It was round and deep and flowing into it was a twenty-foot waterfall; not much more than a trickle, really. While I was staring in amazement, Kelly whipped a tiny Bear Valley spinner across the hole and immediately caught an eight-incher. We let it go, and it was the only fish we ever caught in Cascade Creek.

For some reason, not long thereafter I decided to write a story about trout fishing. The fact I'd never been trout fishing and knew nothing about it was not going to stand in my way. I'd read plenty of trout-fishing stories in *Field & Stream* and the *True Fishing Yearbook*.

So I made up an ideal stream based roughly on an extension of that beautiful pool. I flattened Cascade Creek out and made it into a succession of remarkable riffles, falls and holes embroidered around huge rocks, cool forests and ferns. The sky was clear, the temperature a sublime seventy-five degrees, the water as clear and clean as the spring air after a rain.

It didn't matter that I didn't know how to use a fly rod then; I saw myself moving along this mythic creek, casting a fly in my childish and incomplete, wholly foolish story. The fish were ten-inchers, and even that was an exaggeration of the eight-inch reality I knew. I blatantly offered my imagined readers this fib. I could not have foreseen that thirty-five years later I would actually find this fictional river and it would have ten-pounders in it.

The reason this stream remains protected is that it lies in a largely unpopulated region, and even after going to the trouble to reach this region, it's a long walk getting to it. You can't fly in because of the forest and rough terrain. A hard day's walk takes you to the start of the fishing at the head of a violent, two-mile series of holes, rapids and waterfalls.

I saw the first pool in deep shadow early one morning from a vantage point somewhat elevated and removed from the river. It was just starting to become fall. I stared at it while standing by the fire with my friends Larry, Moe and Curly. At the time I didn't know we were seeing the world's greatest trout stream.

Larry, the titular head of our do-it-yourself crowd, was the first to point out the trout. They weren't that hard to see really; it's just that they were so big you could easily mistake them for rocks or sticks or moss. There were two: the small one would be six or seven pounds, the larger one, a couple of pounds heavier.

This piece of visual information took some moments to fall into focus. I felt for a moment the way you do when you come down the outside of a fast Ferris wheel. I rubbed my eyes idiotically like one of the dwarfs in Snow White. Then the lenses focused, and I was burning a hole in the water, watching the slow movements of these enormous trout.

Sometimes they lay motionless in the crystal-clear water, which was emerald green as a crown jewel in the early morning light. Next they would describe a long oval, perhaps defining their territory or searching for a bit of food. Their world was perhaps one hundred feet long, fifty feet wide and eight deep at its deepest point; not a very large area to support two creatures such as these. Perhaps there were others too, up in the fast water where we couldn't see them.

Taking charge, Larry directed Moe to be the first angler. I was envious, but oddly relieved in a way because I didn't have to worry about blowing what was clearly going to be one bitch of a cast. Luckily, Moe was pretty handy with a fly rod.

Moving into position fifty feet behind the lower fish, which just

Curly.

happened to be the larger one, Moe whipped out a beauty, placing his dry fly half a dozen feet beyond the trout.

On the flat, slow surface, his fly looked like a perky little sailboat. It sailed over the fish, evidently unnoticed.

Larry, who was watching along with us from a respectable distance, called out to advise Moe that he might have to change to a nymph. Moe agreed.

The weighted nymph made the cast harder, but Moe punched it out there and the ugly stonefly landed with a plop. The big rainbow nailed it with the speed and violence Elizabeth Taylor might use in slapping a busboy who tried to reach for her tinkler.

Terrorized, Moe struck, the fly pulled out, and the fish sped to a hiding place. Moe was furious.

"Never mind," called Larry. "Move up and cast to the other one."

This time the fly had time to sink a little before the second trout took with a force equal to that of its poolmate. And, in spite of Moe's every caution, the fly didn't stick this time either.

After a stern debate over hook styles, timing and the fish's heritage, we started upstream. Our route took us some distance above the stream through many different kinds of cactus and sinewy hanging vines which could entrap and strangle you to death if you weren't careful. The others were far ahead of me. For the purposes of this tale, think of me as Oliver Hardy.

Within a fairly brutal half hour I caught up with the boys who were peering over a boulder about the size of an elephant.

"You're up, Ollie," said Moe. "Where the hell you been?"

"My feet were writing a check my heart had trouble cashing."

I could see the fish below the rock. Larry said it was a six-pounder. From downstream I could no longer see beneath the water because of glare, so Larry yelled directions.

I had a handsome little caddis fly tied on, but this fish also refused to rise to a dry fly, so I replaced it with a Trueblood otter nymph. I heard the yells before feeling the fish.

My line slackened, and I realized the fish was coming downstream towards me. I hand-stripped line and the fish glided past, every detail sharp through the aqua water. I noticed in particular the huge square tail. The trout easily took a hundred feet of line before the hook pulled out. We had another discussion.

There was no discernible trail along the river, and again Larry led us up into the thorns. When I caught up this time, the boys were looking down a hundred feet or so into a cauldron of white and light green foamy water. Back where it cleared and darkened, two trout were lying deep down near the bottom. The small one was perhaps a five-pounder, the other at least a couple of pounds more. It was Curly's turn to fish, and we knew he was going to have some trouble with this for several reasons. First of all, he was pretty new at fly fishing. Second, there was only one place to stand to fish the hole and he would have no visibility. Third, the noise of the nearby falls was approximately like that of a 747 taking off, so he would not be able to hear any directions. Larry briefed him and sent him in with a pat on the butt.

It was a painful display. We all suffered with Curly, not because of him. After countless false casts, he managed to lob one up ahead of the fish. One of them seized his fly but because of slack line being pushed at him by the current, he couldn't see or feel the take. And because of the thundering falls, he couldn't hear us screaming ourselves hoarse.

With all diligence, he kept flinging his fly back into the pool. We could see the angst on his face even from far away. Presently, the other fish struck and spit out the fly as had the first.

We gestured to Curly to come up and after he joined us we explained what had happened. He looked like a cross between a man who had just sat on a whoopee cushion and someone whose wife had confessed her infidelities with a third-world sports team.

We walked on, soon arriving at a meadow which was clearly a part of the dream I had three-and-a-half decades earlier. The valley opened up to let in more sunlight. The air was now a sublime seventy-five degrees and the water so clear at times you were almost convinced there wasn't any. The pool was relatively shallow, with a riffle coming into it on a slow gradient. There were at least five fish in the pool, all above four pounds.

Larry, as mentor and counsel, was refusing to take a turn with the rod, so once again it was Moe's turn to be the entertainment.

Two of the fish were holding high in the water toward the tail of the pool. Moe waded to within forty feet of them and laid out an excellent cast. One of the fish took with a slow, deliberate turn to the side. Moe struck, and we all simultaneously cheered as the trout ran forward into the hole at great speed. The hook pulled out and Moe's rod stood lifeless.

A certain purplish tone invaded his face and his speech as he came ashore. We didn't talk much. After all, how much more was there to say about hook design?

We decided to sit back from the pool and have a little lunch. The soft tundra made a good picnic spot. As we munched and chatted, five trout huddled deep in the center of the hole just below a big rock which deflected the current.

Larry asked Moe and me if we thought Jane Fonda would like this river. We shrugged. The talk turned to horses. When we got to dessert, our cookies were covered with ants.

A half hour later Larry said to me, "I believe it's your cast, Ollie. Throw a few flies at this spooked group just in case one of them is feeling better."

I drilled many fine casts here and there, but nothing moved. I think those trout were digging some sort of hole with their fins in order to have a better place to hide.

"Let's get along," said Larry. "If I'm not mistaken, there are *mucho truchas grandes* still ahead of us."

As we trudged upstream, Larry froze much like a heron about to stab a frog. Something was up. He turned slowly to us and addressed us.

"Have a look at this, Ollie. It's still your turn."

There was no pool really, in fact, none. This was a peculiar run strewn with rocks. In one of the troughs was a magnificent rainbow of about seven pounds, hovering high in the current. The trout was all nerves and bestial alertness as it quivered in the full current. It came up and took an insect with almost military deliberation.

This is it, I thought. Nothing can stop this keen, voracious feeder from sipping in my dry fly. Everyone sensed it was a sure thing.

I moved into position, assessed the distance, appreciated the vagaries of the flow, pulled just the correct length of line from the reel and commenced false casting. I was precise and confident until, about three strokes into it, I came forward against solid resistance. My fly was hooked onto an immovable bristlecone pine tree.

Ever alert, Moe rushed to free the line, which he somehow managed to do within a minute or so. Cursing, and more careful now, I started to false cast again but could no longer see the trout.

"Please," I whined to Larry, "tell me where to cast. I can't see the fish."

"He's gone. He saw the movement of you boys playing in the forest back here."

Somewhat soberly, we moved along through a dark avenue of ferns and tall redwoods. What a soft, damp peace there was on this side of the river. Clearly a thousand years meant nothing here, although, when I looked up and saw a vapor trail high overhead, I could feel the hot breath of the twenty-first century breathing down our necks.

We had scanned a mile or so of the river without seeing anything when we arrived at an enormous, rather eccentric pool lying between two awesome, rocky cliffs.

Larry almost did a backflip, screaming, "It's a bloody ripper! My God! Careful, boys. Here, look through these palm fronds." A ten-pound trout and its slightly smaller mate were spied nesting in their livingroom.

Technically it was Curly's turn to fish. Unfortunately, a vicious wind had arisen and was gusting downriver, and these trout were in a terribly tough lie. It would be a long cast into the wind over slow-moving water, and we all knew, Curly most clearly of all, that he simply would never be able to make it.

Moe climbed down into position and waited for a lull in the wind. There wasn't any. It took repeated casts before Moe finally slipped one under the air. The crinkled surface of the water was difficult to see through, but these fish were so big their long, black forms were easily apparent. One of them turned and rushed downstream.

"Strike," screamed Larry, but it was too late. The fish had spit the fly out. One fish spooked the other and both of them made a hasty trip in among the jumble of rocks ten yards upstream.

"Bastards," I heard Larry say as he pulled up his parka hood and started on his way. "We've got to break this streak."

"Well, how about you taking a turn then," I insisted. "We've never seen such fish as these. You're not as nervous as us. I'm not real sure anymore if we're operating with too much hair trigger or in Mexican overdrive."

Not surprisingly, the next pool had a good fish in the tail of it. Larry addressed the situation in no-nonsense fashion. A very competent fly caster, he wasted no time in placing a small black nymph right in front of his target's nose. The target lunged and took. In the confusion which followed, the target elected to go over the riffle back downstream.

"I believe we'll get this one," Larry called out just a moment or two before the hook pulled out. There wasn't much else to do but laugh out loud together.

At this point we heard a yell from upstream. It was Curly, trying to tell us he'd found a real lunker feeding furiously right under his nose. We ran up the side of the river we were on, which was the opposite one from Curly. As we came abreast of him, we saw the fish immediately, a beautiful six-pounder literally slashing flies off the surface.

Curly knew enough to get cracking and it was a piece of cake for him to cover the fish, which immediately grabbed his fly. Moe had sidled up to offer a little advice at his elbow.

It was a good pool in which to play a fish—not too deep, long and uncomplicated by any obvious snags. And here was Curly, who had us worrying that he wasn't having a very pleasant day, firmly attached to the biggest trout of his life, a trout which looked as though it would be the first one landed for any of us.

Curly handled the job very well. He kept the pressure on while the rainbow ran first to the head of the pool, then clear to the tail. Moe, to his credit, did not badger Curly, but rather stood off behind him ready to help if help were needed. All of us were very pleased that this was happening, because the weather was worsening and another such opportunity simply might not present itself. This fish would mean a lot to Curly, and I already had several good photos of him playing it from across the river.

Then the rainbow did a remarkable thing. It ran over to our side of the river, and rather calmly, we thought, circled a rock and broke Curly's leader. I would like to say we all felt worse than Curly did, but that was not the case.

"This is becoming damned serious," murmured Larry. "There are only three or four more pools before the falls. We mustn't be shut out."

The next pool was quite flat and shallow. Larry told me with all certainty if we spotted a fish there, it would take a dry fly.

"A good, honest dry fly will change our luck," Larry stated.

Sure enough a fish was there and rising. We discussed it briefly

Larry.

and unanimously agreed that Curly be the one to fish. This trout looked like another beauty of five or six pounds.

Larry was right beside Curly trying to forge the event to a successful conclusion. After several failed tries, Curly landed his fly ahead of the fish but too far to the right. The trout left its position anyway and executed a bizarre, rolling, slow-motion take. In a moment of uncontrolled excitement, Curly whipped his fly rod back to strike and made one of the most depressing backcasts of his life.

Larry was losing his sense of humor. Perhaps he thought we were blaming him somehow for this ongoing comedy of errors. Maybe he thought Moe would punch him in the nose, or I might allow a grand piano to somehow land on his car, or Curly would slap him and twist his ear, making odd noises emanate therefrom.

Five minutes of reassuring gibberish followed, about how fine it was just to have seen all this, how privileged we all felt to have been led to this most heavenly of rivers. After all, Larry was taking quite a risk: one of us could turn out to be a blabbermouth. Look how close I'm getting.

The next pool was really a jumble of boulders. I stepped up to it with a sense of weariness and resignation, two attitudes I secretly hoped would allow me to catch a fish by accident.

It didn't work. The trout we were fishing for was impossible for me to see, so I cast where Larry told me. He yelled, "Strike," and I did. Need I go on?

Larry gathered us around in a huddle. "Gentlemen, the last pool lies just ahead of us. Moe, you're in the gunseat. I have already seen a couple of rises up there. Put on this dry fly and try to think like Larry Bird."

The situation looked promising. The pool was simple and open, the current perfect, without any obvious treachery, and two trout were feeding aggressively. There was no need for Moe to be the least bit nervous just because this was our last chance and these trout were eight-pounders.

I must say that Moe delivered the goods. We all envied and admired his cast. The fly turned over perfectly even in the gale-force wind and started its jaunty ride on the current. It seemed like an hour before it passed over the fish. Passed over the fish? The fish let it pass?

The fly now rode over the fish's tail and left it like a tiny shuttle leaving the Enterprise. An odd thing happened then, still in excruciating slow motion.

The huge rainbow did a perfect about-face, raised its dorsal fin and part of its considerable back above the surface, and began cruising straight toward the little fly. Moe was stunned.

One seldom sees an eight-pound trout with a mouth the size of Larry Holmes's right hand glower at you as he gulps in a glassful of water along with a Dan Bailey royal coachman. I'm convinced that anyone would have done what Moe did under the circumstances, which was to pull the fly directly out of the fish's mouth.

So there you have it, the horse collar on the world's greatest trout stream, even though at the outset we had all agreed to kill no fish in this river even if we caught one the size of an Electrolux vacuum cleaner. I'm not superstitious either, but if you count my hooking a tree while casting to a sure thing, we had thirteen opportunities and muffed them all.

A number of years came and went. I thought about the stream often, but, assumed I'd never see it again. Lightning never strikes twice in the same spot, right?

For one thing, my interest in the cuisines of the world continued to add extra girth to my person, which was forty pounds too heavy to begin with. The silent explosion could go off any day.

Moreover, I had foolishly become a workaholic, forgetting that all the money in the world can't buy back even one hour of life and that in the last analysis, the largest bill of currency in the universe is nothing at all if you hold it up next to a trout of the same length.

So I decided a two-week vacation every eight weeks sounded like a deal I could live with. Naturally, in between, at least three four-day weekends would have to be scheduled.

You might be asking yourself what kind of job I have and where to apply. This apparently idyllic lifestyle is possible because I'm my own boss; I paint pictures and write stories. Father Guido Sarducci was right—go to an art institute so you can sit around all day drinking coffee and talking about things you know absolutely nothing about.

To get back to the point, my life took a turn for the better. The house was now once again filled with loose tackle, much of it in repair or being built. Fly-tying materials lay about. I tinkered with reels. I went on a diet and lost four pounds.

I managed to set up a trip back to the river after a year of whining, cajoling and begging. The word readiness did not sufficiently explain how things would be handled this time around. I was going to step back into my dream; the trout would be Ginger Rogers and I their Fred Astaire.

I toured the countryside for a week or so until Larry was free to make the trip. With each passing day I felt better and better as I fished dozens of rivers, lakes and streams. I was content and attentive, the best combination of attitudes possible.

When the time arrived, Larry was full of apologies. He couldn't get away, but his son, Sherlock Holmes, would be accompanying me, along with another angler identified only as The Doctor. I was, to put it mildly, terrified that this was part of a vicious practical joke and that my companion might turn out to be Dr. Hunter S. Thompson, who had recently tried to maim me by suggesting I go look at a jeep out behind his house in Woody Creek, a jeep which had been previously loaded with TNT by a group of demented mercenaries. I had been in Aspen to open an exhibition of my paintings and invited Hunter to the opening on the wrong date by mistake. I wondered if he had the cash and the motivation to pull off this kind of revenge. I needn't have worried. The Doctor turned out to be Julius Erving.

It was spring. This time the first pool, which before was in deep shade, lay in bright sunlight. In it Mr. Holmes, Dr. J and I could see two big trout.

For purposes of this part of the account, I need to choose a name. Four pounds lighter, I can be Magnum or Rockford; all right then, Cannon. However, since this is my pen and paper, I choose to be Indiana Jones.

I liked Dr. J right away, and could see that Mr. Holmes was going to live up to his name. I suggested the Dr. fish first. The Dr. operated smoothly, but in this bright light the trout were immensely cautious and moved up into the riffle. Julius was not to be deterred; he put on a full-court press and covered the fast water, where he immediately had a fish on. The river was so clear we could see every detail as the fish came down into the open water. It was a big male rainbow with an awesome hook on its lower jaw.

Julius played the trout resourcefully, and within ten minutes Sherlock Holmes was holding it gently in the water, having removed the fly with his pliers. We measured the fish—twenty-eight inches long, fifteen inches in girth, which, when roughly calculated, came to at least eight pounds.

I was standing on the gravel bar while the others examined and repaired tackle. I cast a nymph almost carelessly higher up in the riffle than where Julius hooked his fish. There was an instant take and a smaller, more silvery trout shot into the air again and again. It made six or eight leaps around the pool and took twice as long to land as the other, even though it was a hen about half as large.

Again we started up into the bush where the pampas grass made going difficult. My being four pounds lighter and having a superb attitude enabled me to nearly keep up.

My memory of the terrain was accurate to seventy percent. Some details were not familiar. When we arrived at the rock where I lost the fish with the big square tail, it appeared to be uninhabited.

Some distance above the rock was a pool half in shadow. Just on the edge of the sunlight a beautiful five-pounder finned over some fine gravel. Julius hooked it immediately and played it into a small backwater, where Sherlock carefully released it.

Once again I stood looking into the unfished shadows and decided to zing in a fly. It was a good idea and a trout was on right away, one almost identical to the last.

After landing it, we walked on and climbed up an ugly face of scree. (I remembered this trek; it was the place I was nearly throttled by some swinging vines.)

We eventually came to the pool where Curly had such a hard time. The 747 was still taking off. We could see no fish, so we moved one.

The lunch pool lay ahead. As we walked I occasionally heard animals moving in the forest but could never see them. They must have been bear, deer, moose, caribou or cattle.

It looked as though there were several fish in the middle of the lunch pool. Julius did a good job casting, but I think they sensed his presence or heard him wading, for they glided into the deepest part of the hole.

I watched a good fish rise four times on my side of the river. Against the sun I could see a halo of spray and mist each time the trout attacked a bug. I pointed this out to Sherlock, who wondered what I was waiting for.

"It's Dr. J's fish."

"You try him," Julius called. "I'm ready for lunch."

I deliberately made this a long cast after seeing how sensitive the other fish were. My leader was sixteen or seventeen feet, so I had a good margin of safety if I overshot. The cast was just right, and the rainbow had only to elevate to suck in the fly. After a ten-minute struggle the five-pounder was safely back in his home, none the worse for wear after being hooked, played, landed, admired and released.

Lunch was delicious, and there wasn't an ant in sight.

We then walked a couple of hundred yards to where I had snagged the tree. I looked it straight in the trunk and told it the Henny Youngman joke about the guy whose hotel room was so small when he stuck his key in the lock, he broke the window.

Meanwhile, Sherlock was lining Julius up on a fish. I had trouble seeing this one, in fact just plain couldn't. But Sherlock insisted and told Julius where to cast.

The take was furious and the fish went haywire, streaking all over the run and finally going over the riffle towards the lunch pool. Dr. J followed with difficulty and in the end landed an exquisite rainbow.

The next little pool had a trout right in the center hovering just under the surface. In a matter of seconds, I had the dry fly on him, he took it and the next thing I knew Sherlock was releasing him.

The next two pools didn't have any visible fish in them on the first trip. This time they did. I climbed around a huge jumble of rocks forty yards above the stream. Sherlock leaned out and stared at the water for some time.

"I see two," he said ducking back from the edge. Julius followed him down to the river while I stayed in the balcony.

The first fish took a dry fly immediately and they landed and released it. The second hung tough until Dr. J showed it a juicy nymph. This one was twenty-six inches long and fourteen inches around.

We climbed on through a rocky gorge. At one spot where the water slowed, we saw two fish. I got into position to cast and, for no reason we could determine, the fish cruised down and stopped right in front of me. I didn't dare move, so I extended the rod and dropped the fly over him. He was caught and released.

Wasting no time, Julius rocketed a cast to the other fish and caught it. Both were roughly four-pounders.

We came to the pool between the cliffs, the one with the two very large trout in it. They were still here, without a doubt the same fish I saw several years before. How long fish live in this water is difficult to say, but fish such as we were seeing could easily survive a decade or more.

I tried a dry fly on them, but they weren't interested. A nymph turned one, and he may have taken, I don't know. It was clear the fish knew something was rotten in Denmark, so we continued on.

According to my notebook I fished the next hole, even though reason said it was Dr. J's turn. The opportunity was such a splendid one perhaps I lost my manners, or maybe Julius was feeling magnanimous. All I can remember is how utterly thrilling the event was.

The fish was not enormous, though still an honest five pounds. He was lying in full view along the edge of a long, slow pool. The sun was shining brightly so that everything was somehow too real, too clear, as in one of those awful surrealist paintings. It was obvious that one slight miscue at this point would spoil everything.

Sherlock and Julius found a spot to the side where they could watch. Seldom does one feel as confident at a moment like that as I did. It never occurred to me that this might not work, so I made the false casts, sensed the distance, and willed the fly toward its mark. It landed eighteen or twenty inches in front of the trout and drifted for three or four seconds until the big spotted nose gently elevated to sip it in. Julius photographed the fish just before we released it.

The next pool had a relatively swift current, which, under the brilliant sunlight, had the sparkle and verve of a great violin concerto.

Mr. Holmes and Dr. Erving located a lovely trout midway in the run and the latter took it on his first cast. They carefully released it.

The pool ahead was the final one before the falls. It was shallower than I remembered, but of course when I saw it last the sky was the color of soot and an ugly gale was raging down the valley. Today, it was literally as peaceful as heaven.

Two trout were lying out in plain view. The water could not be more than twelve inches deep where they sat basking in full sunlight.

As if to celebrate one of the great days of fishing in a life which has been filled with them, I backed off until the distance between myself and the trout was about seventy feet. I was not trying to prove anything. I wanted to take this trout at the outside limit of a number three line, hoping to imprint the moment so it could be recalled someday when lying comatose in the hospital attached to a life-support system with only my tear ducts operable.

It took fifteen years, working at it at least a little bit each day, for me to become the fly caster I wanted to be. I'll never be a ten like Bill Schaadt or Steve Rajeff, but I am a nine, and casting a fly gives me enormous pleasure, equal to swinging a shotgun on a fast bird, and one other obvious thing.

So I pulled most of the fly line off the beautiful little Bogdan reel and started working it. The air felt light, or perhaps there was a two-knot breeze from behind; all I know is the cast was as easy as throwing a baseball.

The fly appeared on the trout's nose and in a moment the big fish was wallowing, stirring up mud from the bottom.

This moment became another thread in a tapestry of the finest silk and most intricate design, a cloth made of experiences which represent the cream on top of a generally milky life. Sometimes when it's very quiet, I sit listening to my own heartbeat, and think about things like this.

Sheridan Anderson, my dear departed friend for whom I frequently mourn, had this to say in his wonderful comic book, *The Curtis Creek Manifesto*. "Is there really a Curtis Creek? Possibly, my darlings, quite possibly; but I will say no more because that is your final lesson: to go forth and seek your own Curtis Creek—a delightful, unspoiled stretch of water that you will cherish above all others. . . . There are few Curtis Creeks in this life so when you find it, keep its secret well."

In closing, I'd like to say to my friend Larry, if he's listening, upon thinking it over, yes, Jane Fonda probably would like the river, although my advice is never to take her or anyone else there ever again. We ought to let something remain.

This is my story and I'm sticking to it.

INNOCENCE LOST

A thousand feet below, the Sea of Cortés lies crinkled by the afternoon breeze. As the Piper Cherokee banks against the formidable Sierra Giganta Mountains below Loreto, I can see masses of birds wheeling near the water, while beneath them great bursts of spray tell of a school of large fish on the attack. Soon we are over a bleached cactus plain west of La Paz where, in the distance, I see the crisp, dark line of the landing strip. Our pilot announces we will be on the ground in ten minutes.

It is Easter Sunday, and the sun flares as usual from a flawless azure sky. In La Paz a radiant throng of people surges along the Maleçon in the traditional promenade, tribute to sweet times and young laughter. And in a different, deeper way I sense the timeless paradox of innocence tested against an almost literary sensuality.

A mild breeze eases in off Bahía La Paz, caressing the bathers and strollers. It lifts the dark, shiny hair of the women and softly furls their finest dresses. The crowd is a kaleidoscope of richly-colored pieces shifting against a broad mural of blue sea.

The mid-afternoon warmth has a certain rightness, an observable lack of insistence. Families jam the beach, spilling up onto the sidewalk where older men and women sit on benches or the curb.

Some seek the deep, cool shade of ancient Indian laurels which grow along a street where a leathery old man sells cold slices of watermelon and fresh coconut milk. Elsewhere along the boulevard, men with pushcarts offer tacos, ice cream or *raspadas*—sweet syrup poured over ice shaved by the vendor from a large block. I am continually asked to look over selections of rings, bracelets, or bits of polished abalone shell. Young boys dart about, anxious to sell gum, candy, a shoe-

119

shine, or last month's Sunday *Los Angeles Times*. One youngster, exhibiting a clear sense of urgency, ducks across the street with a live turtle under each arm. At the water's edge, working slowly, men rake the sand, clearing it of anything unpleasant.

The crowd does not diminish as evening approaches. Instead, its mood and spectrum of color shift to the minor key: dark red, indigo, purple, blue-green. Shadows grow long and fade as twilight hovers over town, striated by the pungent smell of food from restaurants and homes. Dusk increases the flow of Carta Blanca, Tecate and Dos Equis. The hope of intimacy is becoming a promise.

When darkness falls, schools of toro, or jack crevalle, begin to feed, erupting along the bulkheads and sending curtains of minnows into the shallows. The fish are having an orgy of their own, scarcely noticed by the noisy crowd. Across the street in one of the nightclubs a Mexican rock band plays the Rolling Stones' *Angie*. No one will go home early.

For years wealthy American sportsmen have considered Baja their private playground. Resorts like Hotel Cabo San Lucas, Rancho Buena Vista and Rancho Las Cruces were expensive to reach, expensive to stay at, and the guests spent their money to experience essentially the same things: perfect climate, pure, clean air, matchless beaches, a vast sea rich in game fish, wonderful food, and honest, native people.

But when it starts to rain in an arid land, erosion is inevitable. Dollars were the rain, a poor people the dry land on which it fell. And now those first, fortunate American visitors are wringing their hands in despair at the thought of a new highway which will bring a whole new tide of Americans, generally of much lesser means, who will come in an armada of RVs, bringing with them a learned need for comfort stations and golden arches. Louis Bulnes, manager of the tuna cannery at Cabo San Lucas, said, "We are going to lose the tranquility but are going to make a lot of money. Civilization has a price." He may not have fully realized the enormity of unchecked American influence.

The morning air is light and warm. A frigate bird crosses in front of my window in the Perla Hotel, much too slowly, it seems, to be really flying. On the street below, a man tries to start a car without success.

The café downstairs, open to the sidewalk, is busy. Starched waiters deliver plates of huevos rancheros to the tourists' tables. But something is not quite right. The normally robust, dark-roasted flavor of the coffee is but a thin shadow of its former self. This morning, it resembles the hot, colored water you get in many American restaurants. Have Americans, used to their normal fare, been complaining?

And the view of the harbor is gone. Actually it is still there, somewhere in back of several towering motor homes parked in front of the hotel. Their enormous bulk plunges the café into a kind of twilight. Inside one of the larger vehicles, behind an oversized screen of tinted glass, a little girl sits motionless, alone, her pigtails arranged neatly on each side of her head.

The motor is idling, a concession to the air conditioner or perhaps counterpoint to the tour bus parked nearby. In any case, the two of them have teamed up to befoul an entire city block. *Huevos tibios,* orange juice and a large order of fumes, please.

According to the *New York Times* a young Los Angeles man claims to have driven from Tijuana to the Hotel Perla in La Paz in fourteen hours and fifty-seven minutes. Is he here now? Certainly, several brethren occupy a table at the far end of the café. Dressed in heavy black leather, attire as out of place in La Paz as a French bikini in the Brooks Range, eight or ten Americans are lashing into plates of food. Their helmets, slung over chair backs, advertise STP. Their jackets proclaim the merits of Bardol. Their faces show the strain of pointless hurry. The women look like Alan Mowbray in drag. Parked along the street is their transportation: two Harleys, an army jeep and three huge, spare, totally functional dune buggies.

Are they here to get good Mexican food? To enjoy the ladies of the *zona de roja* or the dim, music-filled nightclubs? To dive and swim in the warm, clear water and afterwards lie for hours without purpose on a clean white bevel of sand? To know the people? To hunt? To fish in unbelievable game-filled waters? To write a poem?

***

"The Tourist comes here and does what he is forbidden to do in the States. He feels liberated."

MILTON CASTELLANOS
GOVERNOR OF BAJA

Litter is one of the more obvious aspects of the landscape, as are the tracks of dirt bikes and four-wheel drive machines cutting across dry arroyos and up brushy hillsides.

But some Mexicans seem determined to retaliate, if not precisely in kind. Any number of American tourists have been shot and robbed. Ramon Moreno, the federal director of tourism at Ensenada, said, "We have had to call in federal troops to help our state police in dealing with the situation. There is an epidemic of lawlessness against American tourists along the new highway."

Frequent accidents on the narrow highway have been responsible for many deaths and injuries: more than three-hundred Americans and an unknown number of Mexicans. Still, Americans pour in, bringing their habits with them, driving at unreasonable speeds. The road is narrow for long distances, too narrow for two vehicles, each carrying house, lot and kitchen sink, to pass one another safely; traveling housewives have had to wipe a lot of Spaghetti-O's off the dashboard. Nicknamed "Road of Dreams," Numero Uno is often a nightmare of steep hills, dangerous downgrades, sheer three-thousand-foot drops, unexpected dips installed for flood drainage and an absence of turnouts. Mexicans living near the road have come to call the Americans "crazy gringo kamikazes."

But more than anything else the new highway will explode the twentieth century over a country that has remained unchanged for a millenium. The process is usually called "Americanization," and it has to do with portion control, exorbitant real estate prices and Kentucky Fried Chicken.

Castellanos says, "We cannot stop growth or the progress our people are entitled to." He means the introduction of electricity, telephones, refrigeration, television, imported fresh food and jobs. In the towns, the people covet Sony portables and teenagers wear Hang Ten t-shirts. Lunch at the fabulous new Finesterra Hotel in Cabo San Lucas offers a choice of tostadas or club sandwiches. Many people, including some Mexican tourists, go for the three-decker U.S. favorite.

The electricity mysteriously went out one night in La Paz, leaving the town dark all evening. Business went on as usual, only more pleasantly so, at least in the restaurants and cafes where candles and old kerosene lamps were lit.

In the Hotel Perla, maids nonchalantly passed out candles to guests for their rooms and placed others along the tiled corridors. The atmosphere was almost one of medieval pageantry, the town lit by firelight. Even the members of the electric rock band didn't care. The general lack of concern was something to stand back and admire.

I know where I want to go. There is a rocky punta, then a series of indentations, perfect cabrilla cover. I know this from having cruised the shoreline a few days earlier, studying the bottom, catching many unusual fish by casting a fly near the right places.

Finding it by land is a slightly different proposition. In Baja, certain spaces between bushes, cactus and the bigger rocks are referred to as roads. Negotiating one of these leaves your destination a mystery. Each arroyo is enough like the one before it so that a sudden glimpse of ocean or gulf seems to repeat, appearing suddenly like a flat blue paper cutout.

North of La Paz, the road is paved to Puerto Pichilinque, where the ferryboat from Mazatlán comes in. After that the traveler is on his own. The right turnoff leads to a succession of broad, gleaming beaches and bright, shallow bays, perfect for wading or swimming.

Mangroves line many of the coves, giving them a fishy look, especially when you remember that the world's largest snook live here. At intervals along the way, Mexican skiff fishermen have constructed simple shelters to sleep close to the fishing grounds. Their substantial open boats are pulled up on the beaches. Nets are hung up to dry.

The dirt road I take becomes a nightmare of false starts and once transforms into an ugly sandtrap in which the car buries itself. Then, gaining the crest of a hill, I see a long, deserted beach curving out against a rocky headland. The road veers sharply down, ending in a surreal landscape of white sand and lucent water, a place where sea creatures might appear and reappear as in a dream, divorced from the reality of food-chain survival.

The water looks shallow. But it soon becomes obvious from the steep beach and distorted muting of colors on the bottom that even the shallow places are deep enough for anything except large whales.

I expect cabrilla. In Mexico the term is applied to any number of rockfish along the edges of the Gulf of California. There are several species of true cabrilla, but so many of the smaller inshore rock bass and groupers resemble one another that identification is often troublesome. I can also reasonably expect to hook Sierra mackerel, jacks, snook, possibly small yellowtail and skipjack too, provided the shore drops off steeply enough. In the very early morning or late evening, even a roosterfish will not be out of the question.

At the first rocky point, three Mexican men are fishing with hand lines. I notice them when one stands to cast. They are barefoot, in itself a remarkable thing, for the rock is very rough and the shallow reach of water between it and the beach is covered with a type of small, sharp irregular coral and low seaweed, beneath which there are almost surely hidden a few unpleasant scorpionfish. I stop to watch them fish, looking into a vacuum of time. They coil simple lines at their feet, bait a hook and swing the sinker around their heads, letting it go in much the same way as men everywhere have done through the ages.

I look at my fiberglass fly rod and feel somewhat effete, just slightly absurd. But I want to flycast and have pared the whole business down as much as I can: fly rod, reel, line, coil of spare leader material, a paper envelope of two dozen streamer flies, swimming trunks and a pair of canvas shoes.

Just offshore, there is a tremendous commotion, and I look up to see about fifty small fish clear the water in a ballet of perfect unison, a pattern of silver almonds shooting again and again from the sea. Something large and important is herding them.

Soon I arrive at a fascinating underwater bluff that bulges a hundred yards out with just enough water over it to create a mild surf. At its sides and far end, the bottom drops off into chasms of dark ultramarine. After deciding to fish the shallow roots of the point first, I wade carefully out to the closest dropoff. Nearby, undulating prisms of light decorate the bottom, painting a coral-reef fantasy, where dense schools of brightly-colored tropical fish dart around my legs. Grass and seaweed lean with each surging wave, bending the underwater landscape as if it were a tapestry.

The cabrilla climb over the top of one another to catch the hook. One time, something boils under the fly and hooks itself. It turns out to be a Sierra mackerel, vivid in its coat of orange spots. These fish are all fun, but in the hazy distance I contemplate the light sienna outline of Isla Espíritu Santo, and think of deeper water.

The end of the bluff is not as definitive as it had looked from shore. There is an uneven trough, perhaps thirty feet deep, then a last hump of rock beyond which vast depths call. I decide to sidestroke out there. At the last moment before reaching the rock, a wave pushes me against a sharp coral shelf, gashing my leg and arm and bringing dark thoughts of sharks.

When I stand up I am staring into a frightening hole; even at highest noon the water is dark blue, going to black. This must be one of the most virile kinds of fly fishing imaginable, probing the unseen with a line of thin lead wire.

A long cast seems in order. Keeping the nylon monofilament backing out of the wash by holding large coils of it in my mouth, I ease out a flat backcast and shoot the heavy line high and far.

That is that for the moment; I must let it sink. What strange grottos must it certainly be nearing; galaxies of undiscovered life. Perhaps even now some monster is watching the fly flutter down, a visitor from above, perhaps good to eat.

I start pulling line, and the thirty-yard cast comes back at a steep angle. In a moment there is determined resistance. I sweep against it, leaning into the rod. But it is hopeless from the beginning, like trying to lead a buffalo with sewing thread. Line streams mercilessly into the Cortés, unchecked, until the end is reached and the leader pops like a light-bulb filament.

In the late afternoon on Bahía La Paz, if there is no wind, you can hear the plaintive song of the mourning dove. Crabs scurry around the shallows, frightening pods of tiny minnows. Exposed tidal flats crackle near the mangrove shores.

Across the bay, the city is washed in yellow light. I can see cars moving along its waterfront, especially the larger campers. The sound of a jet engine blasts the stillness as an airliner, rising quickly, leaves La Paz International. Behind it a funnel of wicked, dark smoke hangs in the air for many moments before thinning out in the delicate, egg-shell blue.

With oceanic bonito off La Paz.

DESSERT AS
THE MAIN COURSE

It is dark and the veranda of the Oasis Hotel is cooled by soft breezes easing inland from the Sea of Cortés. Somewhere over in Loreto, dogs are barking. Close by, a young child's voice can be heard near one of the rooms below the dining hall.

"Mom! Mom! I can hear whales breathing."

I shift attention from the fishing tackle I've been preparing to the featureless dark, straining to see what can't be seen. In a moment I hear a heavy expulsion of air, once, twice, three times. Three whales and they're very close. I wonder if they are huge finbacks, the second largest animals in the world.

The moon is about to rise and the sky becomes orange over Isla Carmen. The whale's breathing travels south and I imagine them cruising over inshore ledges, straining sea water through baleen for the plankton they live on. The moon clears the earth in an oblong burst of yellow-orange. The whales are out of earshot and invisible. The only sound left is the gentle lapping of small waves a few yards away.

"Mom, there were whales here, really. I heard them breathe."

"Yes dear. Come to bed now."

In the morning the fishermen go out early. At the Oasis, the guide comes to get me in my room. As I prepare to load gear into the boat, another guest is ready to head out, and without humor addresses his Mexican mentor.

"Captain, I'm really wondering about the gamesters. Do you think we could pretty much stick with the gamesters today?"

127

"Señor?"

"I mean these cabrilla and what-have-you make a nice fish stew and all that, but I'd like to see some gamesters. I want to show these Lefty's Deceivers to something that will burn line. Savvy?"

"Señor?"

The angler takes his seat in the long open skiff and they start out, the forty-horse Johnson straining to push the heavy boat. A hundred yards from shore the boat stops and slowly swivels around. The guide bends over the engine. In a moment he holds a spark plug aloft, examining it against the morning light like Louis Pasteur looking for bacteria in his microscope. The sportsman slumps.

Now it is my turn to try for Isla Carmen. I get a full three-fourths of the way there before the guide decides it's time for a spark plug change. After that it is smooth, if slow, sailing, until spark plug concerns are overtaken by the sight of a thousand wheeling, screaming birds.

"Jello! Mucho jello!" yells the guide. I understand immediately he's not advertising dessert when I see the aggressive boils and splashes of a huge school of California yellowtail feeding beneath the birds.

The guide might be confused by a fly rod but he is matter-of-fact about it, having, I later learn, taken many fly fishermen out to the yellowtail grounds. He knows to cut the engine and drift into the school noiselessly.

The fish are recklessly slashing into bait all around the skiff. I assume the grab will be ferocious, instantaneous. The first cast intercepts a knifing fish. The third and fourth are over strong boils. Panic and loathing begin to emerge as the water around the boat becomes still, each cast appearing to have spooked its intended victims.

Forty yards away another school erupts with a roar. I motion to the guide but he has already started the engine, sending the skiff toward the edge of the new school before shutting down again. I cast with renewed vigor, turning the streamer fly over again and again among clots of seemingly rabid fish. The same thing happens: as each fish is cast to, it vanishes. They know I'm here, I whisper to myself with a sense of paranoia more normally associated with walking across Central Park alone at night. Somehow, they know I'm here. I churlishly and secretly hope that none before have succeeded where I have failed. This is just how it is, I tell myself with a Don Rickles shrug. All the stories have been lies, fabrications flung in the face of hard reality.

Undaunted by failure, the guide unlimbers one of the stoutest boat rods in the world, held together largely by friction tape. With this he flings a huge metal lure, badly straining his reel's gear system. When the jig lands he pays out line for an eternity. When his lure hits bottom two-hundred-odd feet down, he begins cranking and jerking like a crazed warrior around a night fire. Almost at once he grunts and begins pumping a fish. When it gets to the boat it is a smallish grouper. One of fishing's most disconcerting moments is at hand; a fish hauled up out of the depths with its eyes popped out of their sockets because of the change in pressure.

On his next cast, using the same jigging method, the guide catches an eighteen-pound yellowtail. He looks at me inquiringly and gestures toward the water. I have one fly rod equipped with fast-sinking lead-core line so I make a cast and start paying out line. It isn't long before I catch myself at my own folly; it would take the better part of my whole vacation for the heaviest lead line in the world to sink down there. Then what? Even if I hooked something it would go instantly into a cave or else be indistinguishable from a section of coral reef.

The surrounding sea is now flat and polished. Not a fin is visible. Even the birds seem puzzled; they flutter and make false dives at phantom targets. The yellowtail are down.

I point toward the island, and, using voice to inflect the question, ask the guide, "Cabrilla?"

"Si señor. Mucho."

The north end of Isla Carmen is austere and craggy, formidable cliffs facing prevailing seas. Along its shores life is unfathomably abundant, from rocks covered with a kind of sea lice, or *cucarachas de la marina,* as they are jokingly called in Mexico, to coves teeming with fish that defy description.

In the first cove, a school of cabrilla booms to the surface, sending a shower of baitfish up, then down like hard rain. The cabrilla, or snapper, are chunky fish, not very large, but certainly purposeful. They clear the water in peculiar angular leaps, often appearing like dark silhouettes, upside-down, on end, always in outline like paper cutouts.

I roll out some line and shoot a cast into the melee. A fish is on instantly and the dark humiliation of an earlier hour is momentarily

forgotten. Two or three more take a fly even after the school has quieted down and the surface stilled once more.

After this, the guide directs his boat slowly along the shore, stealthily investigating each point and cove. The water is absolutely clear; every nuance of bottom is at hand, every fish in plain view. I alternately troll and cast my fly, hooking any number of cabrilla. Once I see a green sea turtle hugging the bottom, flippers outstretched, head cocked to watch the skiff pass. I point excitedly and inform the guide, "Tortuga!"

In halting English he says he has not seen a turtle in a very long time. I recall that as long ago as the turn of the century, a thousand green sea turtles were being shipped every month from lower Baja to San Francisco. Now they are all but extinct. Even here in this dry, nearly uninhabitable forsaken land, this frontier, all is not well with Mother Westwind's children.

One resident of Loreto, an American who retired there for the fishing, speaks sensibly and matter-of-factly. "They used to say the Cortés grouper, the big ones, fifty, sixty, seventy pounds, were inexhaustible. Now those giant grouper are a thing of the past. There's still lots of grouper but they're smaller. Hell, those big guys are forty or fifty years old. How many of them can you catch and still expect there to be more?"

With respect to the yellowtail the story is a bit different. Migratory creatures, they spend the winter in the region of Loreto and Mulegé where food is abundant. They are never really being pulled from their living rooms as are the resident bottom dwellers. Yellowtail are an interesting fish for saltwater fly casters because they are pelagic, living and feeding largely close to the surface. Much like tuna, they are built for tremendous power and speed. This fact can also make them hard to catch. Unless yellowtail are already in a feeding frenzy, it is nearly impossible to interest them in something as slow moving as a streamer fly. I suspect as well that while in a calmer mood the fish are quite cognizant of fraudulent baits.

That evening on the pier at Loreto a knot of people are gathered, watching several young boys fish. The youths take their fishing pretty seriously, seldom smiling or joking among themselves. Each has a length of monofilament line with a lure attached. This he swings about his head, letting go so that the line coiled at his feet follows the lure far out into the bay. Each also has a smallish pile of fish.

A man I met earlier at the hotel is on the pier and walks over.

"Say, aren't you the fellow with the fly rods? Why don't you try it off the pier? Catch all kinds of fish."

"What kind are they?"

"You name it."

"I can't name them. I've never been here before."

"This is the place for those fly rods. These little guys here."

For a moment I think it might be fun to try but I don't; the boys are making what for them constitutes a living off this pier. They aren't sport fishing. I consider the morning's frustrations and for just a moment think the man is right; the fly rod is for the little guys. But then I remember why I came to Mexico.

The morning is a carbon copy of the one before: perfect, cloudless sky, windless. Off the beach near the Oasis, pelicans are soaring and diving into schools of tiny fish. In formation, five or six of the big birds veer and fold in unison, twisting toward a chosen target. The baitfish are small, an inch to an inch-and-a-half. How is it that such large birds are interested in such small prey?

On the run to the fishing grounds a tremendous school of porpoises passes the boat. The hundred or so mammals dive sharply under and around the skiff as if inviting me to join them, wherever they're going. In the distance I begin to see the birds sparkling in the morning air like precious gems. Looking through my tackle an idea surfaces: could the yellowtail be feeding on tiny baitfish like the pelicans? I find a small silver, blue and white bucktail about an inch-and-a-half long and rig it on a long, absurdly light leader.

Just as he had done the previous day, the guide cuts his engine and eases into the yellowtail, which feed at least as furiously as before. Today though, several tiny baitfish skip out ahead of some powerful swirls. With determination I false cast the shooting head until several boils appear near the boat. I drop the fly on them and pull fast. Instantly the water seems to careen and bulge and instead of retrieving line I am losing it straight down.

At the sound of the captain's voice I turn; he is grinning broadly, showing some gold. "Bravo señor! Jello!"

AN ANGLER'S
AFTERNOON

Yellowstone Park at the beginning of the season is like a museum when it first opens early in the morning. Visitors are scattered, often lonely types, wandering among the paintings and sculpture, the creeks and pine trees. They know the lack of distracting crowds makes the time more important, the impression more lasting.

If you want to walk into the back country to go fishing around the first of June, count on being there well ahead of almost everyone else. At the campgrounds only a few hardy tenters sit around their fires. The familiar crush of people at Old Faithful and the bumper-to-bumper "bear jams" are still several weeks away.

I'm here to catch a grayling, the Park's most distinctive fish, not only in appearance but because of the altogether tenuous hold it still maintains in a few remote waters. Aside from that the general stream season opens on May 28, a date that's early spring at this elevation. Going early is wise because later the mosquitoes will be intolerable.

No ranger is on duty at the North Gate near Gardiner, so I stop at Mammoth to pick up the required free fishing permit. At 7:30 on this crisp morning the community is relatively deserted and I have to search a bit to find an employee.

The exhibit building is open. Inside, it is well-heated and several workmen are arranging ladders to paint the rooms before the tourist season gets fully underway.

A representative from each form of wildlife found in the Park stares glassily from cases placed around the room. I wonder for a moment how it would be if instead the cases were filled with an attractive arrangement of politicians or administrators, all labeled, while wolves strolled around the corridors.

133

In the last room a ranger who's just come on duty is watching the seismograph. Eerily, it records a minor earthquake over in the Bechler River country. He gives me a permit and a copy of the regulations which, among other things, says, "Killing or possessing grayling is prohibited." And there is a simple line drawing showing the fish's singular silhouette with its high, saillike dorsal fin. This expedition will not be for the sake of the banquet boards.

In half an hour I stop near a bridge over a fascinating, serpentine little river. This is where the walk begins. After leaving the road, the trail skirts a meadow, then climbs into the woods where the sound of traffic is soon lost to the wind in the evergreens. Soon the wind in turn is drowned out by a high falls, above which the grayling live. Tall shafts of silver light filter to the forest floor and design stark, bare spots around deep drifts of snow. There are tracks of marten, deer and elk but, as anticipated, no human footprints. Blazes along the trail are dim after a long winter season in the bitter 10,000-foot elements. The trail leaves the river to cut across several ridges and in about an hour and a half slopes sharply down. Once again I begin to hear the jingle of rapids. Walking in hip boots has been less than ideal, but when I reach the river they serve their purpose as I cross and recross it.

I find a small, bright meadow and decide to sit and prepare my tackle. As I relax on a bed of fragrant pine needles I am astonished by a tremendous heaving and flashing in the nearby riffle. A female rainbow trout of easily seven or eight pounds is spawning. I see her clearly as she intermittently turns on her side, thrusting to dig a nest. The male hovers behind her. Though small by comparison, even he will weigh a substantial five pounds. I sneak in above the fish and float a nymph again and again past the trout, but they show no interest whatever. I think of a clever solution to the problem and tie on a tiny silver-bodied fly. But the flash of silver merely frightens the huge rainbows into the protection of deeper water where they become invisible. This is poetic justice as it is bad manners to interrupt spawning fish in the first place.

At intervals along the river, mineral-rich warm springs flow from the canyon walls. The flora around them appears fluorescent; a multitude of miniature flowers and fernlike plant life are gathered near for nourishment. It is these springs, so characteristic of the Yellowstone plateau, which prevent certain small rivers from freezing solid during extended periods of thirty to fifty degrees below zero weather.

Since it is too cold for most insects to be hatching, I drift a weighted fur nymph through likely places as I walk. Several hundred yards from where the trail first bisected the stream, I catch a two-pound rainbow. Dark and vividly red along its side, it is a spawner like the first two big fish, probably down from the lake. I catch and release several more from the same run before going on.

The river is in sparse woodland and flows in tight curves, offering an endless number of interesting runs and cut banks. The rainbows are coming with astonishing regularity, at least one per pool and sometimes as many as three or four. They are good fish, too, averaging a pound with some nearly three times that.

Above, another meadow promises. I am now in what the French call the *zone à l'ombre*. The most precious reach on any stream, the grayling zone is the cold, clear headwater, an impeccable habitat.

The population of grayling in the United States, outside of Alaska, has been reduced to token numbers, with the fish confined to a very few remote Rocky Mountain areas. The upper Big Hole River in Montana has grayling, and some are still found in Utah as well as other parts of Wyoming besides Yellowstone Park. Grayling are fished for in much the same way as trout and thus the two become associated. Actually grayling belong to the salmon family, though the similarities are not particularly recognizable to the lay eye. In character, grayling resemble the mountain whitefish more than anything else, but the whitefish can tolerate less than ideal water conditions while the grayling cannot bear any impurities. Aside from a similar appearance, especially their terete shape, the two species are alike in that they thrive well even in the bitterest temperatures. Both feed actively during the cold winter months.

Now the river divides the meadow in tight switchbacks so that in a straight quarter mile there is perhaps twice that much water. A textbook stretch for the dry fly, and I regret it is not precisely the weather or season I'd have ordered for dry fly fishing. It is alternately raining and snowing a wet slush. Nevertheless, when I approach a dark, interesting pool where tendrils of last year's watercress and moss wave in the current, I am greatly encouraged by a rise. I study the broadening rings which the current sweeps back toward me as if there might be some mistake. The wind has lulled, though large snowflakes, which vanish when they touch the back of my hand, are still falling. I replace the nymph with a small gray bivisible.

Hoping for a grayling rather than a native cutthroat or another rainbow, I'm pleased to see the fly line slide truly toward its mark as the fish rises again. The fly drops perfectly and naughtily cocks itself this way and that as it floats over a grassy ledge. There is a splash and it vanishes. The line curves sharply back and when I've taken up slack, the fish characteristically shimmies away with a series of bronze flashes. This is my first grayling, a rare event even in this wilderness. I embellish the moment by comparing it with seeing wolf tracks or glimpsing a mountain lion before it rushes into the forest.

Soon the fish is on a hummock of earth and I carefully remove the fly from its tiny mouth. Before turning it back, I can't resist raising its spectacular dorsal fin, the way everyone did in all the pictures in all the fishing magazines I ever read. Released, the grayling seems to soar down out of sight beneath a bank of moss. I catch several more at different pools until the sky closes over and the wind renews itself to confound casting. I decide to start back.

The bank of the river is essentially swampy. Unpredictable too, as part of it suddenly gives way beneath my left foot. I'm in just slightly over the boot, enough to funnel half a gallon of ice water down around my toes. Up until now I've ignored the downpour, which has become steady, the time, and the fact that the trail head is more than a mile away. I've passed the point of no return on that score and now must walk out along the river. Allowing for its drastically irregular course, it will be a five-mile walk.

The question of making it before dark arises. Unfamiliar with the trail, I recall the words of an old-timer neighbor: "You won't get lost if you just remember that the snow gives you your up and down and after that you just follow the river."

I arrive back at the car somewhat hysterical with fatigue. An empty creel is a testament to the quality of my day. It is nearly dark and snowing steadily. A camper passes slowly as I peel off layers of wet clothing. The sound is muffled, a little like scotch tape pulled slowly from the roll; its tracks on the smooth white road look almost mystical.

When I have turned the car around and started tiredly back, I see five elk grazing at the edge of a meadow, where the pine forest stands dark and fertile and promising. This has been a day that will be easy to remember.

Releasing a steelhead on the North Umpqua River.

WINTER STEELHEAD FISHING

The Basics

This morning the fog is hanging close to the redwoods and firs. It is the middle of December, several days after the season's first rain, and wetness is implicit everywhere: on the shiny river stones of the gravel bar, on the heavy, drooping marsh grasses, and among the ferns, in the ocean less than a mile distant, in the sky, hanging against earth like a great damp coverlet, and in the river itself, green, but not emerald, softened by the mist and morning light to a more inviting tone.

Where will the steelhead be today? At the end of a long bend just above tidewater I see the grayish, indistinct forms of fishermen already in the water. A closer look suggests these men are not strays, but serious fishermen. They are not fooling idly with their equipment or chattering among themselves. In fact, they seem a bit ferocious in their endeavor, one they obviously have in common, and one in which I wish to share.

I wade cautiously out above the last of the five men. He turns and nods a greeting, but says nothing. With a firm sweep he rollcasts his fly line out of the water and makes several long, smooth false casts before the rod hisses a cast so far out over the river that the landing fly is nearly obscured in the fog.

Below me (below the fisherman, actually) and out in the river perhaps twenty-five or thirty yards, a great fish erupts against the surface with a sound that is almost guttural. The rise is quick yet implacably powerful, and the anglers murmur as each offers his own particular prayer.

A half-hour passes. The river is cold as it presses in on my legs and feet. Half the time, my casts tangle and collapse and I must try again. Even when they lay out reasonably straight, I suspect they are many yards too short. I'm having trouble with the monofilament shooting line, which seems to foul up no matter what I do; I bring the fly in to check it and find three knots in the tippet. After tying on a new one, I drop the fly into the river and wonder if I should change patterns. When I try to rollcast, the fly is caught in the monofilament. The first time I hang the bottom my heart leaps. I decide to try a new pattern after all and tie on another fly. Several casts later that fly is lost, too . . . and the tippet. My heart no longer leaps when the line stops.

As the morning passes, the choice of flies becomes dictated by what remains in the box. The nearest angler appears to be having none of these troubles. He makes the same sure, sweeping casts he slung when I first arrived. He is not shivering. He doesn't constantly check his fly. Some of his casts are intimidatingly long, some are shorter. Sometimes he angles them downstream, sometimes straight across. His energy seems entirely focused on the water.

Fierce envy is added to frustration when he comes up on a fish, and I watch, grief-stricken, as the huge steelhead crashes out of the water, then knifes crazily just beneath the surface. The angler backs out of the water to follow the fish upstream, his reel literally shrieking. My attention is taken entirely by the contest, though I pretend to be fishing with more enthusiasm than ever. Upstream, the man's line angles far out into the river and I long to feel my own tighten and surge with life.

A quarter of an hour later, far upstream, the man beaches his fish and comes walking back down, carrying it by the gills. Appearances forgotten, I reel in and wade ashore, wanting nothing more at the moment than to view the creature close at hand.

"How big is it?" I blurt out dumbly.

"Oh, twelve pounds, maybe. About that."

"What did you get him on?"

"Fall Favorite."

And, unable to think of another question, I gaze balefully at the beautiful fish, so bright and silver it seems to shine from the beach like a light, while the man wades back into the river and starts fishing again.

When I first started going steelhead fishing about thirty-five years ago, the one and only thing I wasn't short on was advice. Some of it was awfully good, most of it was outright moronic. It took a full ten years to separate the wheat from the chaff. And after that, while there were always new situations and difficulties, it became the new simplicities that satisfied most, a new simplicity being a sudden amalgamation of former tangents into one whole segment of understanding.

Perhaps the most essential change in my own attitude came when I no longer considered the game an adversary, nor saw fishing and hunting in terms of contest or challenge. It became more appropriate—and it goes without saying, a good deal more satisfying—to participate rather than compete. Strangely, I began to feel this way about the time I achieved a fair degree of proficiency; in other words, about the time I started to know what the hell I was doing. And that is the only rationale or the only excuse I can offer for the following advice.

If you are going to fly fish for winter steelhead, the very first item of tackle to consider is the line. It must do two things: reach the fish, and put the fly on their level. Obviously then, the qualities of weight and specific gravity need to be considered. A no. ten line is standard. A nine or even an eight might put you in the picture part of the time, but do yourself a favor by choosing the ten.

One line is not enough. This is the single instance in acquiring tackle where skimping is a big mistake. Winter steelhead are not always sitting on the bottom like rocks, nor will a fisherman always be in water of the same depth and current speed. Without lines to match conditions, how can you reasonably expect to catch the fish? Three lines are essentially necessary: one that sinks slowly, another that sinks moderately fast, and a third that goes down very fast. A fourth and fifth might be added—a floater and a lead core—but for starters, these are unnecessary. To fish very near the surface, use a slow sinker, a long leader, and a buoyant fly. For depth, fish with an extra-fast sinker, a short leader, and a heavily-weighted fly. Extend this principle for the sake of argument: if for some reason you can only buy one line, the moderate sinker should be the obvious choice, since you can modify its use by varying leader length and fly weight.

After the line, or lines, select the rod. The choice is between bamboo, fiberglass, and graphite. If you are just getting started, you won't have developed any preferences and the real consideration is money. It is not axiomatic that the more you spend the more you get. Bamboo might be the best choice for a trout rod, even for a beginner. But a bamboo rod substantial enough to cast a no. ten line will be brutally heavy, heavy enough to tire even an experienced caster. It's not the actual casting that will be so fatiguing; remember that you have to hold up the tip weight and it takes a long time to catch a steelhead.

That leaves the practical choice between glass or graphite, and there are many available models in both. If your budget is limited (and whose isn't?) start with glass. It's possible to build one for about $40 plus two hours of time. If you lack the time or the inclination to do it yourself, buy from a reputable maker whose rods sell for around $100.

One of the most common errors beginning fishermen make is to believe they must have an expensive fly rod. As a result they often try to find a rod that will work for steelhead as well as, say, bass or even big river trout. This is a consequential error. Steelhead tackle is steelhead tackle. If there are any fly fishing clubs or casting pools in your area, be sensible and quiz those who already have some equipment.

Choose a single-action reel that operates smoothly. Again, it need not be expensive. Unlike trout, steelhead will always be played from the reel, so purchase something with sufficient diameter to take up line rapidly, and conversely, to give it evenly.

Now, to the casting. I have to digress here a moment, having earlier taken perhaps too much for granted. The type of fly lines needed are thirty-foot shooting heads, or shooting tapers as they are sometimes called. Their design and subsequent use dictates a mode of casting very different from that used to cast "whole" ninety-foot lines. The shooting head was designed for steelhead fishing, where long casts are usually needed.

Ideally, practice casting on water, preferably at a casting club where there is a pool with distances marked off. This will show how the casts are landing, which is quite important. There will no doubt be other casters there who will be happy to help should you want or need assistance. When practicing, use a leader and fly (the hook clipped off, naturally) similar to what you would fish with. Familiarizing yourself with how the casts are turning over will be very important on the stream. From the casting platform, or standing on the ground, you should be able to cast one-hundred feet with some consistency before even thinking of going fishing. That same one-hundred-foot cast under controlled and artificial conditions will quickly shrink to around seventy-five or eighty when wading belly deep in the river, dealing with a breeze and otherwise understandable excitement—not to mention fatigue, which will set in far earlier than expected.

It won't take long to realize there are an astonishing number of fly patterns from which to choose. Convince yourself that steelhead, in common with all other fish, are unconcerned with and know nothing about fly patterns. People joke about "flies tied to hook the buyer." Avoid getting hooked. Steelhead never take any particular pattern of fly. Upon occasion they may, however, take a type of fly, and of these, there are four: large, small, bright, and dark. Within these categories the arrangement of materials and colors is 100 percent irrelevant. Choose patterns which appeal to you, ones in which you can develop confidence.

After doing some fishing, you will begin to know what type of fly is best under different conditions. Obviously, low, clear water calls for something small and subdued. After a rain, when the water is high and milky, use something more substantial. With experience, you will come to attach less and less importance to a specific fly, and concentrate more on how and where it works.

Aside from the tackle, buy chest waders. Hip boots will almost never do on streams of any size. Putting yourself in position to cast is a most important part of steelhead fishing, so buy the highest waders possible. In addition to good waders, get functional rain gear and quilted down or Dacron long underwear. If you are wet and cold, your interest in fishing quickly disappears.

Thus equipped, you are now ready to look for the big guys. Steelhead invariably lie in the same type of water, whether the river is in California, Oregon, Washington, or British Columbia. There are three places to seek: long, even riffles, the tail ends of pools just before they break over the lip, and the pools themselves. Fishing the fast water at the head of a pool will almost never be productive for winter fish.

Where the steelhead lie is directly determined by the height and clarity of the water. Remember too, that these fish are migrating, motivated by the need to spawn, and their movements are dictated by the condition of the stream. Looking at a hypothetical river from the season's beginning to its end will roughly establish certain predictable patterns and situations. The main winter runs will arrive from about the middle of December to the middle of January. A few fish may come in sooner, as early as the first of November in some rivers, and many streams have strong late runs in March and even April. In timing particular rivers there is absolutely no substitute for local knowledge.

Some smaller coastal streams are blocked at their mouths by sandbars, which build up during the summer months when freshwater flows are at their lowest. A rain will usually open such streams for the season, or if the rains are late or very light, gradual freshwater buildup may break the bar. Naturally, inland streams, like those that flow into the Columbia, never have such a problem.

The flow of the river will determine what the fish will do immediately following their entry into freshwater. As a rule they will spend at least some time in tidewater or in the lower pools, acclimating to the stream environment. If there is a tidal influence upon the water where the fish are holding, this will affect the fish's inclination to strike as well as where they will hold on different stages of the ebb and flow. As a rule, the ebb offers better fishing, possibly because it re-establishes the river's normal movement toward the sea, and also because it encourages the fish to adopt relatively stationary positions in the current. Milling fish are often hard to catch.

Another point worth mentioning is that if these lower pools and lagoons are shallow, with gentle currents, this is the place to apply the slow-sinking line. Often, especially in lagoon situations where there may be almost no current, and the fish circle and mill about, a high, rather brisk retrieve of the fly often gets results.

Let's suppose that it has rained and fish have moved into the lower pools of the river. Then it stops raining. When the river is dropping and has gone to a light shade of green, the steelhead will strike with relative abandon. As each day passes, the river drops further and becomes clearer, and the fish become harder to catch. They edge toward the deeper pools, easily frightened now, and are extremely wary of lures and even large flies. To catch anything at this point, lengthen and lighten the leader, and begin going to the smaller flies.

Then it rains again. Wait for the river to start dropping once more, and know there will be more new fish below, while the others have scattered upstream. There will come a point, and it will vary from river to river, when the main runs have all entered the stream. If the water has enough volume, soon most of the fish will be up in the tributaries spawning. It won't be long before you begin catching spent fish returning to the sea. If they have not had to go too far, they will still be quite bright and in strong condition. Still, most anglers turn such fish back, hoping they will come to spawn again next year. Spent fish are usually thin, but even if they aren't, the bottom of their tails will reveal a slight abrasion from having scraped gravel as they hovered closely over their redds.

It is safe to say that steelhead lie in the deeper pools only when clear or otherwise low water conditions move them there for protection. Under normal conditions, when flows are strong and the water a bit off-color, they will always favor the tail end of the pool. Here, there is usually a bit of a dip in the bottom where they may settle to avoid the heavier current flowing above. This is especially true of those pools where a steep, difficult riffle lies below, causing the fish to need a rest after passing through it. Such dips are often used for spawning as well.

Steelhead, which are nothing more than a migratory strain of rainbow trout, share with the resident stream rainbow a love of fast riffles and a characteristic quickness. Even winter fish, slowed down somewhat by cold water and sheer size, often move to take a fly with amazing speed. It is almost always more productive to retrieve the fly rather than simply let it drift without any imparted motion.

The system for fishing a piece of water is reasonably simple. Starting as high upstream as fish may be holding, wade out to where you can cover the water and begin with short casts, gradually lengthening them until you reach your limit. Control the depth of the fly on its swing by changing the direction of your casts. Angle them upstream and the fly will go deeper; angle them down, and the fly will ride higher. When the fly has settled to within sight of the bottom, begin retrieving so that it swings in an arc below you. Takes may come at any point during that swing, up to and including straight below. After your longest cast, take several steps downstream and repeat until all the potential water is covered.

The depth and speed of the current determines line choice. You want to be able to fish the fly clear around below you without snagging bottom, yet work it within a foot or eighteen inches of the same. The right line in combination with the right cast direction will accomplish this.

Another peculiarity of the steelhead, one shared by salmon, is that they often reveal their positions by rolling at the surface. If you see a fish roll, try to get into position to cast to it as quickly as possible. Remember to allow for the current. The fish is not on top; he swam up from the bottom and then returned there. Get upstream from where he showed and let the fly float into his apparent lie.

One of the least appealing gimmicks used to get the fly down to the bottom is one where lead wire is wrapped around the leader knots or cinched around the line where it joins the leader. Unfortunately, this is sometimes necessary in certain British Columbia streams where the water is so intensely cold that the steelhead will hardly move from the bottom. Luckily, this maneuver, which pretty much puts an end to decent fly casting, is seldom needed in coastal waters.

When trying to locate fish, it is unwise to spend a great deal of time fishing one piece of water. If you work through a stretch twice without seeing or hooking anything, move. If you found fish one day and they are gone the next, try to relocate them upstream. The old-timers used to say steelhead in a traveling mood would go about four miles a day. Year in and year out, that's about right for a night's progress, providing the water is neither too low nor too rough.

While you are always delighted to hook just one steelhead, stumbling upon a bunch of them is better. This is usually easiest in the lower reaches of the stream, because as the fish move up, they tend to pair off or divide into threes or fours. By the same token, after spawning, the fish tend to regroup into schools again as they begin to migrate back toward the ocean.

Fly fishing for winter steelhead is as difficult as angling gets, if for no other reason than the season. The weather is nearly always cold and wet, and many hard hours will have been spent for each fish taken. A day on the steelhead stream does not make a nice family outing. This is a sport for fanatics.

Fishing Mill Bend on the Gualala River.

CUTTING IT DOWN
TO SIZE

Years ago, there was a saying in the West to the effect that if you fancied yourself a distance fly caster you had better be able to hold your own among the boys at Singley Pool. Although its contours and even its exact location changed with each winter, Singley was the best and usually the most reliable among the lower Eel River pools.

The first year I fished there the pool was enormous: 100 yards wide and 300 yards long. It was the end of October and an early run of winter steelhead had just come in. The king salmon were thick, too, and the silvers were just starting. In the gloom of early morning fish were rolling everywhere. At the lower end of the pool fly fishermen had waded in from both sides, and although most of them could cast 100 feet or better, the river was wide enough to prevent crossing lines with a person on the opposite side.

My companion, Frank Allen, had loaned me a couple of lines because all I had was dacron, a material which sank far too fast for this slow-moving and shallow water. One of the lines was something called a half-and-half, woven from equal amounts of dacron and nylon. The other was all nylon and huge: size AA, which is about the same as a no. eleven on the modern scale. This line was rubbed with graphite; rather than floating, it would just break the surface tension and sink very slowly.

I waded in as deep as possible without submerging my elbows and did my level best to cover the water. To my left was the late Joe Paul, a tremendous distance caster who had taken the trouble, some years earlier, to give me some instruction in casting. He was using a nine-and-a-half-foot glass rod and a thirty-five-foot no. eleven shooting head.

149

With a powerful and exaggerated double haul, he was covering an un-believable amount of water. On his better casts he was fishing at more than 120 feet.

The point of all this was to catch dream fish: huge salmon and steelhead just hours out of the ocean. Singley is a transitional pool, being, at times, the first pool above tidewater, or the topmost tidewater pool, depending on the height of the tide. These fish were the hottest possible, taken before the water got cold enough to slow them down.

My first fish was a small king salmon of about eight pounds, called locally a chub, a term applied to any male king under, say, ten or twelve pounds. It didn't matter; it was big enough for me. The next fish could be a silver or king chub, a half-pounder (the name for any summer steelhead under about three pounds), a mature silver, a twelve-pound steelhead, or a forty-pound king.

The big kings were the most fascinating of all, being strong enough to overpower the heaviest fly tackle. Many were hooked but few were landed. Some of the older fishermen viewed these monsters with alarm and, when they hooked one, simply pointed the rod at it, grimaced, and broke the leader.

There can be no specific definition of where a medium-sized river ends and a big one begins. Maybe, as with a rattlesnake, to see it is to know it. But two things are certain: no one can wade or cast across it. In many cases casting a third of the way across will be impossible and the current will be too powerful to step into above the knees. You will feel small.

The lower Eel is a big river. Its size has to do with the linear distances one must cast to cover the water. The river is very placid in the fall before the rains of winter roil the water and flood the banks. Many of the pools are far too large to be fished by wading, and casting from an anchored boat becomes necessary. The pools are broad and still, winding among bright green meadows and flanked by gravel bars thousands of yards long.

Large concentrations of fish pile up in the lower river before the first winter rains move them upstream. They show up well in the clear water, and the habit of rolling also reveals their position.

The principal skill needed to successfully fly fish the lower Eel is distance casting, especially on the lower pools down around Fortuna.

Modern distance fly casting originated in California at the Golden Gate Angling and Casting Club of San Francisco. As soon as tournament casters put together the first shooting head, fishermen at the club saw immediately how perfectly suited this new innovation would be to steelhead and salmon fishing.

At the time, which was about 1950, the hot line was a three diameter one made of silk, called the Marvin Hedge Seven Taper. With this line, an expert, under ideal conditions, could expect to reach out to about eighty feet while he was wading waist deep. When that same expert went fishing with the new shooting head he found himself casting another thirty or even another forty feet with somewhat less effort than it took him to cast eighty feet before.

Today distance casting has become very sophisticated, especially with the development of strong, lightweight graphite fly rods. A fiberglass fly rod nine-and-a-half feet long and powerful enough to cast a no. eleven line would soon wear out even the strongest caster. With graphite, fishing with a ten-and-a-half-foot rod becomes comfortable because it actually weighs less than a nine-foot glass rod designed to cast the same weight line.

There is a fairly large difference between what can be done with a no. nine and a no. eleven. Even within its own definition, distance casting is varied in its application because rivers themselves vary. Three things must be considered: wading depth, fly size and wind. The one constant factor is that it is illogical to use any other style of line than the shooting head, more commonly known as a shooting taper.

Assume you will be wading waist-deep most of the time. This means there will be no dropping the back or forward casts. It also means you will have to become adept at handling the monofilament shooting line to keep it tangle-free. The best system is to hold loops of it in your mouth. Standard steelhead patterns will be size four and in some cases, size two. Flies like this are best cast with a no. ten line or larger. Conversely, if you plan to go down to size eight's or ten's while attempting a long cast with the ten line, only weighting those smaller flies will produce a decent turnover. Finally, count on it being windy. All things considered then, a fly fishing outfit for distance casting is a no. ten or larger.

***

Despite this discussion of distance casting on big rivers, a kind of river exists which we shall not call big, but rather enormous, on which a long cast is exactly the wrong thing. These include a couple where steelhead fishing is good, the lower Deschutes and the main Clearwater. These streams have tremendous volume, are generally wide, and largely unwadable. They make the Eel look like the Old Mill Pond.

What to do? First, put away your distance casting outfit. Forget about the middle of the river. These rivers are so heavy there is only one way to fish them: along the edges. You won't be needing a sinking line either; the currents are generally too fast for that. The most interesting runs of fish in these streams are summer steelhead, and they are highly inclined to hit a surface fly.

As a rule the percentage of fishable water on very large rivers is quite small, seldom more than ten percent. While distance casting is the basic skill on a broad, slow stream like the Eel, knowing the edges fish will hold to becomes the most important thing in fishing gigantic water.

With regard to steelhead, only experience will teach you where they lie. Certain runs on certain rivers are productive at certain times, and only sound local knowledge can dope this one out.

Fishing a greased line for steelhead is a very effective tactic, as different from sinking-line fishing as night is from day. The sinking line is rather more difficult, because on the one hand you face a problem in trigonometry—current speed relative to depth, and how to get the fly to the right place at the right time—and on the other hand you must imagine or visualize the situation correctly. Greased-line fishing is one dimensional; you have only surface currents to be concerned about. Nevertheless, what the method lacks in terms of mental nuance it more than makes up for by providing thrilling moments at the time of the strike.

Perhaps more than other kind of fishing, it is in trout fishing where the big rivers are most intimidating. Trout fishing is an intimate pastime in tradition and practice. Still, some storied rivers of the West lure the trout enthusiast out of Michigan or Pennsylvania, and bring him, of a summer, into Montana. It's not that Montana doesn't have any small streams. It most certainly does. In fact, the small streams are very often better than the large ones. But few can resist at least one try at the lower Madison, the Yellowstone, or the Missouri.

The first time I went down into the Yellowstone canyon below

Tower Falls I didn't have the foggiest notion what to do. I was with my neighbor Wilbur Lambert, who knew exactly what to do. After watching him catch about ten trout to my one I began to get the picture. It was those old devil edges again.

The cutthroats in the canyon, in common with trout everywhere, feed as close to shore as they can while still leaving themselves an avenue of escape back into deeper water in case of danger. Wilbur is an agile and tireless rock-hopper, an invaluable asset when fishing water that is 100 percent unwadable like the canyon water of the Yellowstone. He knows how to spot likely pockets, eddies and changes in current speed, and his short casts are deadly accurate. And he does it without falling in.

Even after the Yellowstone broadens and slows below Gardiner and on as far down as Big Timber, the edges are important. Drift fishing is both popular and effective and a good boatman will keep you within comfortable casting distance of those all-important banks.

There is another way to reduce this kind of big water to size. The Yellowstone, Madison, Gallatin and the Missouri Rivers, to name just a few, are often broken up into channels, and it is not at all unusual for a small side channel to provide infinitely better fishing than the so-called main river.

In the fall when the browns move onto the spawning beds, anglers who fish the Yellowstone and the Missouri begin to think less of the edges and more about casting big streamers over broader, more even runs. Most choose the shooting taper to do this. Even so, this is not quite the same kind of fishing as steelhead or salmon. You'll do best by keeping an eye to those side channels, looking for the disturbed gravel which marks the redds. Even in more open situations, the controlled cast is more effective than an undershirt-tearer.

Finally, there are some rivers which are not only big, but also deep. The Smith River in northern California sometimes holds king salmon at depths of twenty-five feet or more. It's a very specialized situation, calling for a very specialized bit of tackle: leadcore fly line. A few years ago you had to make your own leadcore shooting heads out of trolling line. Now several companies manufacture them.

In any river you care to name, large or small, there are places where there are few fish and places where there are many. And in some other places there are fish which are hard to catch because of tricky currents,

153

a difficult approach, or very heavy angling pressure. No matter what the water, you never just fish anywhere you want, but fishing a big river isn't as restrictive or intimidating as it first appears. It's simply a matter of learning to find those places where the river will allow you to fish. Each different river tells you in its own way. All you have to do is listen.

The peanut gallery on a coastal stream.

SALMON ON THE FLY
. . . OR ON THE RUN

Long the sport of kings, fishing is just what the deadbeat ordered.
                                        THOMAS MCGUANE

If you are at large with a fly rod in the Pacific Northwest and want to catch some salmon, particularly the big kings, there is one alarming matter of which you will want to be apprised. By legal definition, Pacific salmon are not classified as gamefish but rather as food fish. The implications become clear on the stream: the club, spear, gang hook and dip net are at least as popular as the fishing rod.

I was with some friends one fall on a stream not far from Portland. There were silvers in the river but recent rains had muddied the water and it would be several days before it came back into shape. One man who knew how to handle his casting tackle caught two fish and we engaged him in conversation.

"If you want those big slobs," he said, referring to king salmon, "head over to the Trask. It's full of fish. I got my limit there yesterday morning. Quite a deal to rassle one of them big ole thirty-pounders. I only fish for them to get my steelhead bait. Three big hens keep me in bait most of the winter."

None of us had the slightest interest in obtaining bait; we weren't much in the mood to kill a salmon even if we caught one. A river full of fish, though, was a magnet. The Trask, like other nearby rivers, is a clean, brilliant stream which drops quickly out of the heavy timber to broaden as it winds among dairy farms just above tidewater. It is precisely the right size for fly fishing and has a pleasant and interesting blend of pools and riffles.

Our man had suggested a place to start. The directions described a certain farm, a tin can conveniently located to deposit a fifty-cent trespassing fee, a dirt road to the river, and finally, a large pool packed with salmon. He added that he had never heard of anyone trying to catch salmon with a fly rod.

At daybreak the first morning at least forty cars were parked at the end of the dirt road. More were piling in behind us like traffic heading to the ball park, their headlights stabbing erratically at the sky as they negotiated the deeply rutted road. At least fifty fishermen were already trying their luck in a hole that common sense said would only hold six.

Upon cursory examination the environs were strictly depressing. A labyrinth of well-worn trails strewn with trash led down to the river. Once there you faced an unfathomable amount of additional garbage: discarded lure packages, cardboard bait containers, food wrappers, rags, beer and soda pop cans, and an altogether dangerous amount of snarled monofilament. Covering it all like the finishing touch on a bad practical joke, or the icing on the cake, was a vast, matted layer of salmon eggs—discarded bait—combined with white powdered borax. The borax is used to preserve roe, giving it a tough skin so it stays on the hook. When dropped on the ground (an apparently mandatory detail), it lends the scene an ambience only to be otherwise found in the most ill-kept laundromats of east Los Angeles.

Talk from along the river sounded unfriendly, comprised largely of hostile bursts of profanity. You could have taken it for a chain gang tearing up trees with stubborn roots rather than people fishing.

Upon leaving—which, it goes without saying, we did without uncasing the rods—one of our party slipped on some bait and landed in a pile of borax, spoiling the seat of his pants. People still in the process of rigging up glared as we turned the car around to go. On the way out the tin can was so full of change people were stacking their four bits on the ground.

The day was beginning to look like a fright wig, so we reconnoitered over breakfast. Maybe we could find some harder-to-reach pools where there would be room to fish.

In Tillamook, the town nearest the river, fishing fever was clearly in the driver's seat. Nearly every car had fishing tackle in it and muddy fenders. Citizens routinely strolled around in waders, shopping or going to the barber. It was obvious from bits of conversation overheard on the street and in the restaurant and stores that absolutely everyone fished. Those unfortunate enough not to be on unemployment did it before work, at noon instead of eating lunch, and after work before it got dark. The level of solidarity in this community was enough to make any politico blush with envy.

Later in the morning we stopped by the Highway 101 bridge. Cars were parked on each side of the road in long lines. Bait and borax covered the road shoulders and even the road itself, where passing cars left behind long smears. A row of people, mostly loggers in hard hats, dangled an assortment of lures into the river. Upstream at another bridge a sheriff was needed to direct traffic. The day was turning sunny and warm, which evidently brought out even more people. Such weather in Oregon is something like summer in the Arctic: in those years when it happens at all, it's usually on the Fourth of July.

There were definitely salmon in the river. I watched several big schools come over the riffle below the bridge then disappear into the pool. The pool was a beauty, ideal for fishing a fly, had there been room. Judging by the fish I saw come into it and the number of rolling salmon, there were possibly fifty to seventy-five fish holding; about one for each fisherman. The river was visibly dropping and clearing. Under the bright skies, with every conceivable fishing implement bombarding around their heads, the salmon huddled on the bottom. They would not bite.

This, however, did nothing to dampen the enthusiasm of the thundering herd. The beach was filling up. Two families had brought playpens, complete with babies. Picnic equipment and the inevitable package of boraxed bait were set up alongside. At one point one of the babies reached out and helped himself to some soapy salmon eggs. The hardier fishermen wedged themselves across the river where the bank was rocky and steep. Since the river was only about seventy feet wide even the most inept caster could throw far enough to snag the opposite outfit. Given a liberal benefit of the doubt, there were at least two, and sometimes as many as ten, lines crossed every second. Absolutely no one was fishing at all.

It was indeed becoming a gathering of strange bedfellows. Several people had brought down their in-laws to watch. Some were quite old; one man appeared to be in his nineties and had a cane. They brought a chair down for him. An old lady walked slowly along the gravel bar in a black hat and black coat, looking as if she ought to be feeding pigeons in Central Park. There were half as many onlookers as there were actual participants. There was so much discarded monofilament that running children often became entangled, going down cleanly like South American cattle hit by bolas.

We were enthralled. If they could package this and ship it to Beverly Hills it would be an Art Event to raise the most jaded gallerygoer's eyebrows. It would be the talk of the town, more astounding in its implications than the laser-beam show at the Hollywood Bowl. The Arts Council of Century City proudly presents Sunday Afternoon on the Trask River, starring the Original Cast of Complete Nincompoops.

One man didn't have any trouble at all with regard to tangled lines. He arrived on a Harley chopper. He had a surf rod. He was dressed in black pants and wore a black t-shirt advertising the heavy-metal rock group KISS. On his hip, gunslinger fashion, he wore a .357 magnum. A gorilla wouldn't have been given wider berth.

Finally, one woman hooked a fish. It sawed back and forth, putting up a terrific struggle when taking into consideration the saltwater rod, the forty-pound test line, the completely tightened drag, and the two other people helping her hold the rod. Several people entered the water holding long handled nets and gaffs. The thirty-pound fish gave the folks their money's worth for a good fifteen minutes before it was dragged up to the playpens. On close examination this salmon had not had an easy life. It was scarred from some early encounter with a seal, its mouth was deformed from having torn loose from a commercial line at sea, and it had a big treble hook in its dorsal fin. In fact, the lady hadn't caught the salmon at all; her bait had merely tangled in the treble hook. This salmon had been yanked from the current like a bad comedian from the vaudeville stage. It hadn't even opened its mouth.

A lot has been said about catching big king salmon with the fly rod. But almost all of it has been about the Smith River in northern California. It's true the Smith is a perfect stream, but if all the people who want to fish land on one river, you get the same thing you do when you rub two sticks together: friction.

Another common bit of advice is that lead-core line is necessary to catch the fish. Naturally, there will be some times, as in any kind of fishing, where lead line is just the ticket. Nine times out of ten, though, lead line will be as useless as a fur coat in Panama.

Of all the salmon in the world, including steelhead and sea-run trout, my favorite is the king salmon. Why this is so may not be easy to explain, or, it may be very easy to explain but hard to understand. They are the biggest and the strongest; I'm the last to deny the appeal of those traits. Steelhead and Atlantic salmon move quickly for a fly in fast water. King salmon don't. Nevertheless, the king is a more aggressive fish and often takes more readily than a steelhead, especially in slower water. Because of their great size, kings aren't flashy. They don't foolishly expend energy. When they turn for a fly it is with determination. The difference between fishing for king salmon and steelhead is like the difference between shooting Canadian geese and doves. All are great sport but they are very different. I love to hunt dove and I also love to fish steelhead but I am much more astounded and awestruck by geese and salmon. Therefore, I have to say I like them better.

Each person's temperament and preferences vary. For instance, if given the choice I will always choose to fish slower rather than faster water. It suits me better. You can approach the situation more flexibly and it's easier to see what's going on. And the casting is a bit more demanding; there's no ruffled surface or swift current to muffle a clumsy slap of the line or straighten a badly turned leader.

Fly fishing for king salmon is not a popular sport, and it's not likely to become so for quite some time. It's too difficult. I don't mean to say the fish is inherently harder to catch than any of the other salmon or steelhead. It's just that most of the potential fishing places haven't been discovered yet. Atlantic salmon fishing in any one of a hundred European rivers has been thoroughly scoped out before you or I were born. People have been casting flies there for a couple of centuries. They know what time of year the fish run, how they move during various water conditions, where they hold, and what sort of flies they respond to.

Along the Pacific Rim—from Japan up through Russia, Alaska, and down as far south as California—there are literally thousands of rivers running salmon well into the billions, yet only a dozen have ever been fly fished for their salmon. And of those, only two or three have been fished thoroughly. If you wander around Oregon, Washington and British Columbia you will be hard-pressed to find anyone who accepts the notion that king salmon will take a fly at all.

This fishing is so hard, then, because you are always starting from scratch, left to your own devices with regard to timing, finding a suit-

161

able river, and locating the pools where fish will hold. On top of all that you have to avoid the kind of crowds that make fishing unpleasant, if not downright impossible. Even though fly fishing is largely unheard of, plain fishing is often out of hand. Local fishermen throughout the West found out long ago that all the Pacific salmon, and steelhead too, can be caught on almost any kind of bizarre gizmo they care to throw in the water.

The same is true of Atlantic salmon. Only because of that fish's long-standing reputation as a gamefish and its popularity with wealthy and influential fly fishermen has such boorishness been traditionally, and often legally, against the law. On the West Coast, suggesting that the rigged anchovy, the Glow Puppy Spoon, the Buzz Bomb, or Cherry Drifter might be inferior to a size ten fly fished on a greased line will get you, at best, uncomprehending stares and, at worst, a punch in the nose.

A fly fisherman seeks fish fresh from the sea. The season is not very long. Once the salmon cease feeding and begin to mature sexually, they darken in color and their flesh deteriorates. The fish should be left alone in this condition so they may go about the business of spawning, which is why they come to the rivers in the first place.

There are two runs of kings, one in the spring and another in the fall. The spring-run fish generally come to the larger, longer rivers. They travel to the spawning grounds in April or May, rest and mature there all summer and spawn in the early fall. There is only about a month during the time when they first enter the river when they are bright enough to fish for.

The fall-run fish may begin showing as early as the middle of August, depending upon the latitude of the river. In some streams, the Smith for example, the main runs come in during November, with a few fresh fish coming in as late as the first of the year. In this case, bright fish can be caught in the lower river any time from the first of October to the end of December.

Low water is the most interesting for fly fishing. In fact, nothing except a fly really works during low water. Still, several conditions are required before fishing can get good. The most obvious of these is that you need a lot of fish. During periods of low water the percentage of fish that are takers drops. So you need more fish to work over. Secondly, it's important the fish be reasonably concentrated in a riffle or pool. A little wind to crinkle the surface or deep water where the salmon feel secure doesn't hurt either. The final necessity is a lack of heavy sinkers and large flourescent lures. This last is often the hardest to come by, because where you find salmon you inevitably find heavy tackle boxes.

As with all migratory fish, fly patterns are irrelevant. If the water's clear, salmon will take anything that's not too large. When the water is up and a bit on the greenish side, anything up to and including a banana will work. Methods of fishing are much like those used to catch winter steelhead. Sometimes you want a floating line, other times a lead core. Figure it out.

The solution to the crowding problem on the rivers of the West is not in sight, largely because most people don't view it as problem. They not only don't mind a lot of company, they prefer it. The conclusion you inevitably reach is that people are essentially gregarious and that, given a choice, they will always exercise that tendency, imposing it on all their activities no matter what. For instance, when you are alone in a skiff twenty miles off Key West, totally isolated and looking for tarpon, another boat will rivet your attention to what its occupants may or may not be doing. In the long run, what the competition is doing is as interesting, if not more so, as what the fish are doing.

Even among trout fishermen, a notoriously finicky and lonely breed, those who like to fish alone are a distinct minority. On Henry's Fork in Idaho or the popular stretches of the Madison River in Montana, most of the fishermen are from out of state and are attracted as much by the presence of other trout fishermen as they are by the promise of good fishing. Not only is a crowd desirable, to them it's essential.

I don't happen to believe in public fishing without regulations, at least in those instances involving precarious resources. You might define a precarious resource in several ways: it could be a fragile population of fish, a delicate environment, or in a larger sense, a pristine one. In my opinion the Trask River mentioned earlier has been utterly pillaged by the local citizenry. It is a garbage dump, treated entirely without respect as are its runs of fish. The reason is that it is wholly available.

In Yellowstone Park bait fishing is not allowed at all and a portion of the water is restricted to catch and release fishing. It seems nothing short of a miracle to me that such rules were ever enacted in the first place, let alone enforced. Yellowstone is a public park and may be the single largest tourist attraction in the country, yet because of rules, which on the surface appear to discriminate against the majority, most people's normal fishing habits are outlawed. The results are clear: Yellowstone Park has some of the best trout fishing in the world within its boundaries, and much of it takes place in complete solitude under the noses of a million visitors a year. The restrictions, enacted by the few for the long-term benefit of the many, instruct the public that there is something here worth preserving and protecting. You don't see trash on the stream banks of Yellowstone Park.

The environment on many of the rivers of the West is not essentially any different than that which you can see any day on upper Broadway in New York, Market Street in San Francisco or Sunset Strip in Los Angeles. Just because people have gotten used to it and the younger fishermen have never known anything else and therefore accept it as normal doesn't mean it's right. The fishermen I've known for the last twenty-five years, who looked forward to fall and winter as the time to think about salmon and steelhead, have all done one of three things: given up the sport in disgust, accepted crowded conditions with a shrug, or cleared out. I belong to the latter group, having no interest in viewing the remains.

The time will arrive, and it can't be too soon, when you will only be able to fish certain coastal rivers by special permit. This is how big game hunting is handled in the Rockies, and the reason there are still lonely, pristine rivers in Europe, a continent that has been overcrowded for ten centuries. When you hunt antelope in Montana your name is drawn at random and you are given a special tag to hunt in a designated area. A lot of locals whine that more than seven hunters could hunt in zone A, for instance. But the seven hunters never caught so much as a glimpse of one another, shot their antelope, had a high-quality hunt, and there are still vast herds of antelope grazing in zone A. It is exactly as simple as that.

Perhaps someday a few of the salmon rivers of the West will be similarly protected from the assault of thieves, snaggers and gunslingers. Given a few hard winters the laundry detergent would be washed away and thoughtful fisherman could then enjoy and protect what is rightfully theirs.

With a thirty-pound striper from Richardson Bay.

NIGHT MOVES

There is a shallow arm of San Francisco Bay, which, during the twenty years I lived in the area, was within ten minutes of my house. The place was so spartan, so unappealing in the light of day, so geometric and outwardly perverse, that fishermen overlooked it entirely. If you had pointed it out to a trout fisherman he would have wanted to throw up.

As a striped bass fisherman I saw something else. Looking for special purposes beyond the inexcusable damage done by industrial and civic disregard, I found a place to catch bass as large as thirty pounds or more, by fly casting from shore.

At that time, in the early- to mid-sixties, there were plenty of stripers, and many different places to fish for them. I literally did so every day from about 1955 until 1970, when I moved to Montana. During that time the fishing did nothing but improve. This secret hole was a pleasure largely because going there was not expeditionary. It was a little like having a spring creek winding through your yard.

A look at the tide and current tables gave a starting point: low tide. From there I determined the part of the flood I wanted to catch and at what time. There was room for two fishermen. But this was one of those fragile, precise situations which defined the thinness of the line between failure and success. Success here meant fishing a very exact edge of the current at a certain hour, and from one angle in particular. At the time it seemed gravely important that absolutely none of this data fall into the wrong hands, i.e, the hands of anyone who ever even vaguely considered owning a fishing rod.

Now, urban life has never been known to dull the primordial urge to fish. I know one New Yorker, the author, Nick Lyons, whose excellent and popular prose more often than not deals with the conflict between his need to be a city dweller in order to make a living and his strong desire to spend time alone along quiet waters. Others, like Guy DeBlasio, armed with a large billy club and matching cajones, take their light tackle of an evening and head straight for the Harlem River.

In San Francisco, which is to New York what fresh *linguine alla Vongole* is to rat poison, I frequently saw people loading tackle into their cars in the early morning, especially in the quiet neighborhoods. Most stayed close to town, fishing from piers, beaches or rocks. Others went to the waterfront to take a boat out on the bay or ocean. Still others, depending upon the season, went out of town an hour or two after steelhead, salmon, trout, shad or black bass.

Some of the men were construction workers, some had desk jobs at City Hall, some were Montgomery Street brokers, bankers or executives. Others worked in department stores, restaurants, banks or shops. A number were elderly or unemployed and lived in buildings now toppled in the name of urban renewal. It didn't matter. A phone call to someone with a screening secretary was put through twice as quickly if it was about fishing than if it had to do with actual business.

There was something to be said about finding one's sport close to home (excepting, of course, an illicit session of the horizontal mambo). Brochure esthetics and the often outrageous outdoor magazine promises invariably failed to compare with the rich skein of knowledge which results from simply paying attention at home.

I remember one evening some years back when a friend and I had all the luck in the world at our secret hole. We had decided a new ruse was needed *vis-à-vis* concealing the car, and ended up leaving it about 600 yards away at a commuter bus stop. It was after dark as we slipped over a low embankment to start the fifteen minute walk through weedy, uneven marshland and acres of debris. My friend had a pair of black waders, the kind so popular in New Zealand, a black parka and a black wool stocking cap. When I kidded him about face paint he replied that someday I was going to give the whole thing away by wearing loud clothing like my snot green sweater.

The cool evening air was unusually still that night. It was not, however, in any sense quiet, and we had to converse in voices loud enough to be heard over the heavy drone of nearby traffic. Around us the landscape was complicated, inorganic, industrial; piers, bridges and docks gave way to frontage roads, restaurants, service stations, office buildings, apartments, condominiums, and a galaxy of night lights.

When we reached our destination—a complex of pilings just a few yards out from the muddy bank—the tide was slack low. We sat down on a large pipe, in all likelihood a sewer, to wait for the flood to begin. Nearby was a sharply curved offramp which, to judge by the constant squeal of tires, most cars took a little too fast. As we sat talking, there was a sharp screech of rubber against asphalt and a tremendous crash. Within minutes the highway patrol was there, red and yellow beacons flashing, reflecting off the water and freeway abutments like a sixties Fillmore Auditorium light show. Soon a tow truck was tacking into position near the twisted metal and broken light filaments, as police radios crackled loudly in the night.

We both saw the figure moving toward us along the pedestrian walkway. It seemed preposterous to make a run for it like fugitives, and there was really no place to hide. There was simply nothing to do but stand up and start walking casually as if it were the most normal thing in the world to be strolling around under the freeway in the middle of the night in waders and carrying fly rods.

"I think we're safe," I whispered. We tried to look as inconspicuous as possible. "This guy looks drunk as a skunk to me."

And drunk he was as he passed by without even acknowledging our presence. But his reaction was merely delayed.

"Hey! You guys!"

We stopped and turned slowly.

"Been fishin'?"

"Uh . . . sort of."

"Get any?"

"No."

"Yer doin' it wrong. It's the wrong night. C'mere. Yer gonna think I'm blowin' smoke at ya. You think I'm blowin' smoke at ya I know, but I've seen 'em *this big!*" He jabbered, and held out his hands to indicate a large fish.

"Now, I'm drunk. I been drinkin'. Okay. But I swear I'm not makin' this up. I've seen 'em jumpin' by those pilings."

My friend and I looked at each other, both thinking the same thing: was this how the fickle finger of fate was going to deliver our secret into the hands of the public domain, through this blabbermouth telling everyone who would listen about big fish jumping all over the place just minutes from the tavern?

"I know, I know," he went on holding his hands and arms outstretched in a gesture that made him look like he was supporting a leaning panel of plywood with his fingertips and forehead. "You guys think I'm blowin' smoke at ya. Believe me now, second full moon of the summer. Warm night. Be here. See, the mosquitoes fly down by the water to keep cool, and the big fish are right there waitin' for 'em."

We laughed and thanked him for the terrific advice, and enthusiastically convinced him we didn't think he was blowing smoke at us. Seeing we took him seriously seemed to give him great pleasure. We promised to return at the time of the second full moon (whatever or whenever that was), but only if he agreed not to spread the news further. He went on his way, humming.

Back at our station the tide began to move. In the wake of some pilings, distant lights glinted off tiny folds in the current. As the water gained momentum, bits of food would be dislodged and small forage fish disoriented. When the tide reached a particular pitch, we hoped to see the first feeders explode out on the dark edge of the channel as the predators sensed it was time.

A patch of reasonably intact marsh lay near where we fished, its light green grasses lush and dense. A wooden structure built at the turn of the century still stood at its edge. Something old did remain. The years had laminated their influence upon the countryside, but certain places were covered more slowly than others; some not at all. This phenomenon is a bit like fattening a picture over the underpainting; paint and repaint, yet in the end certain areas are finalized by being left alone. You lose the habit of rifling through the pages of time, perhaps because mental health rests in some large measure on coming to terms with the present. So, oddly enough, it took me a while to realize that the "secret riffle" as Myron Gregory used to call it, was mere yards from where my mother and her family lived in the early decades of the twentieth century.

They lived on a houseboat, one of many which then lined the little slough. My grandfather, Gottardo Piazzoni, a painter, did sketches of the arks, the bay, and the surrounding hills. Rich paintings, soundly constructed and sensitive in every detail, which recorded moods of solitude, peace and warmth. These beautiful works gave no notice what-soever of the coming of condominiums, freeways or the Army Corps of Engineers.

But come they did. The two-lane country road and wooden draw-bridge were replaced by ten lanes and soaring overpasses. The arks, simply yet elegantly built by ship chandlers, were easily smashed into flotsam by the massive blades of efficient D9's. Dissatisfied with inti-mate, serpentine creeks and sloughs, the Corps dredged and straight-ened every mystery out of them, leaving behind bare, evenly beveled shores unfriendly to herons and mallards. The landscape was given a giant manicure, polished off with apartment complexes, shopping malls and a seemingly endless number of fast-food establishments.

Oddly enough, at the time there was still something intact about the water itself. After a century of increasing pollution, public indig-nation had finally begun to turn the situation around. People were not only calling for an end to indiscriminate dredging and filling of the bay's shoreline, but were also demanding that neither industries nor cities be allowed to release untreated waste into the water. To every-one's astonishment, about a decade and a half ago the bay was cleaner than it had been for sixty years. Biologists discovered forms of marine life on San Francisco's waterfront not seen there in more than half a century.

At the same time, the population of striped bass was far larger than it had ever been. Runs recorded by the durable Leon Adams in his long-standing classic, *Striped Bass Fishing in California and Oregon,* began to reappear after having been nonexistent since Truman was president.

In 1965 I caught nearly a thousand bass by fly fishing, killing only about a dozen of those. Then in 1966 I was lucky enough to land a thirty-six pound striper which became a new world record on the fly. The previous record—a twenty-nine-pound striper caught by the late Joe Brooks—had stood for eighteen years. All reasonable leads panned out: there didn't seem to be any place where you couldn't catch bass.

Before long, a small fish hopped erratically from the water, hotly pursued by a striped bass. My friend landed a cast in the right place and had a take immediately. His fish pulled to one side, giving me room to cast to others which had begun to feed. My streamer was soon hit and we were both connected to struggling fish. We landed them and made a bed of rushes to hide them in the dark.

It was a good night and the bass fed wantonly, visibly reckless as they slashed into an endless buffet of bright silver smelt. Within two hours, four more stripers were hidden in the reeds. The smallest weighed at least fifteen pounds, the largest about twenty-five, our lawful limit. In any quarter it was a very impressive catch, made all the more so by the difficult and arcane craft of fly casting, and taken under the noses of ten-thousand speeding cars while we fished in a kind of solitude as complete in its own way as that of the Canadian Rockies.

We decided one of us should get the car so we wouldn't have to carry everything so far. It was late enough that few people were around. Just as everything was put away, headlights beamed over us, then a spotlight. The patrol car pulled right up behind us.

"Be cool, it's nothing," my friend advised.

Two officers got out, and the first said, "Sheriff's department. Everything okay?"

"Oh . . . well . . . uh, we just thought we'd stop for a little air, walk around, look at the water, you know, get outside."

"Here? You boys have some identification?"

We gave him our driver's licenses and the second officer took them to the car.

"Kind of an odd place to be getting air isn't it?" the first deputy said, looking at us, then at the surrounding area.

"Officer," my friend began earnestly, "maybe we'll get into less trouble if we just level with you. We were shooting a little pool at that bar about five blocks from here when we decided to step out and smoke a little number, you know? Didn't think we'd be bothered down here."

"You have any more stuff in the car?"

"One joint was it."

The second officer came back with our licenses. "These are okay."

"You guys get out of here now, and don't be hanging around down here anymore."

After they'd returned to their car I said, "Good Lord, why did you tell him that!"

"Look," my friend explained, "a lot of cops like to fish. They're like firemen. They all fish and hunt. Suppose those two deputies happened to be fishermen? If they found out about this spot they'd go crazy. They could even time their rounds so they could get in a few

172

casts right during the best part of the tide. That would be it. You know how touchy this place is. I had to tell them something they'd believe, something to completely satisfy their curiosity."

"What if they arrested us for drugs?"

"They didn't, did they? And we don't have any, either. If they had wanted to make an issue out of it we would have had to tell the truth. But they didn't."

Rudi Ferris with a twenty-pound striper at Stinson Beach.

PUMPING
IRONY

The first light of dawn was beginning to show over the grassy ridges, summer yellow even in the morning darkness, when I entered another kind of gloom: fog, pushing up the canyon from Bolinas Lagoon, threading its way among the eucalyptus groves, diffusing details, making the road wet and shiny. Like reentering a more silvery night, the fog was a silent dream, a promise of solitude.

The surf: certainly one of nature's finest edges. You can see it as the end of land and the beginning of the ocean, or the end of the ocean and the beginning of land; it really doesn't matter. What does seem to matter is the intensity of its rhythms and its rather explicit statement of timelessness.

In the fog I was relieved of vistas. There was no point in looking for the horizon, the Farallone Islands, or looking back along Bolinas Ridge and Mount Tamalpais to watch the steeply-beveled slopes flare into brilliant cadmium yellow. I could barely see across the channel to Stinson Beach, and Duxburry Reef lay well outside my field of vision. The fog was elemental, still and heavy; the sea, washing thinly up the beach, was mercurial, restless, endless. As I walked into it my footprints disappeared quickly in the water-soaked sand.

Into my dome of silver light the bass came slashing carelessly, sending showers of anchovies into the air. I saw the fish as distinct individuals appearing momentarily in the foam, or in the face of a wave. The fly rod seemed much less out of place than it did earlier, because the first fish of the morning was taking line with him down the channel, into the open surf. I was thrilled by such long, straight runs.

More bass came to the fly, almost too eagerly and time was lost. Hours passed. The tide had hissed its way completely out and that cycle was over. The fish withdrew to quieter waters and the flight of sea pigeons became aimless and ceased to have meaning.

Stopping later for coffee in town, or what passed for town, because on that day when I fished twenty years ago Bolinas was pretty sleepy, reminding me vaguely of New England rather than California, I could have quite easily convinced myself I was living in another century.

The party had gone on until about 3:00 a.m. so there was little point in trying to get any sleep. I'd planned to be up at 5:00, on the bay by 5:30. Several cups of coffee made me into a wide-awake drunk with a headache.

It was November and the bass were thick around the Richmond-San Rafael Bridge. So thick, in fact, that the previous morning I'd caught something like fifty, and the bite lasted for nearly three hours. Put simply, it was a fish a cast. Party or no party, I wanted another such morning.

I was stuporous as I brought the little boat down from behind the Cable Crossing sign near the blockhouse at San Quentin. The bay was slick. Another quiet morning. Over at Point Molate the usual fires flared, compliments of Standard Oil. Dawn colored the sky faintly rose.

From just a few yards offshore to as far as I could see, bass were boiling. They weren't big, averaging maybe five to eight pounds with the odd fish going to twelve or fifteen. I cut back the tippet to a truly crude twenty-pound test and flattened the barbs on several flies and a couple of poppers.

The first fish took on a five-yard roll cast. After that, variation took over: casting across the tide, uptide, behind pilings, in front of them, under the bridge, on the other side in the wake of the bridge. I even perfected a technique of skinning the fly along the top so when a bass came after it I could tease it away from him and play with him awhile.

Even poppers lost some of their thrill; even with barbless hooks, there was still the matter of pulling the fish to the boat to release it. Finally, after catching fifty or sixty bass, an idea came to mind: I took a streamer fly and cut the hook off about three-sixteenths of an inch behind the barb.

I made a long cast and had a grab immediately. After a few seconds of solid tugging, the hook naturally pulled loose. Another fish took it. The second fish came off just like the first. I could work two scams: pull the fly fast to get a bunch of fish teased and following, then when most of the line was in, let a bass grab. He'd run the line back out, get off, and I'd start over. I mentally recorded well above a hundred takes on the hookless fly.

Even while the bass were still feeding I'd had enough. A real grownup's hangover had the upper hand, and I knew the bass would still be there the next morning.

A bright and sunny midwinter day, with no wind, gives me a most peaceful and encouraging feeling. I used to look for such days in those years when the stripers wintered in Tomales Bay, waiting for the big outgoing tides, mainly because the fish's movements in falling water were reasonably easy to chart.

We knew the bass liked about four feet of water and they'd move to maintain that depth. We used blind casting to find a school but I learned to accept those spaces between fish as essential counterpoints to the more specific, active moments.

I remember fishing a glassy afternoon early in January. A few trollers were fooling around off Millerton Point but I knew they were in trouble. The water was cold and the bass lethargic; I was getting gentle boils behind the fly every six or seven casts, potential strikes a troller would fail to see as he motored his lure away from the very bass he hoped to catch.

I always assumed two things when fishing Tomales: that if I showed a bass my fly at all, he'd make a try for it, and, when I got a solid grab, or just a boil, that fish was not alone. The former conviction made blind casting an acceptable system; the latter conviction let me locate schools of fish rather than just strays.

I always fished from an eight-foot boat, one of those designed like an El Toro sailer so I could row it quite fast. The system for locating fish was to drift over the approximate territory I thought they'd be in, and make a cast to this side, then that. I was handling about seventy feet of line, so each drift could be considered to be a probing swath 140 feet wide. With any amount of bass in the area at all, I didn't go too long without a grab.

Quiet evenings on the low water were always my favorite times to be on Tomales. I worked up a religious feeling about those twilights which I cannot, even now, begin to describe. Even though the air was usually cold, dusk seemed to settle around me like a warm bath. It was quiet and blue, indistinct, like looking into a dark pond.

There were fish right up until dark, and often a bit after that, although the real excitement disappeared with the last light of day. But by that time there was usually a fish or two in the boat and the long row back across the bay gave time for the day's events to settle and become comfortable in the mind, like new flooring in an old house.

During the ten years between 1956 and 1966, when I fished for bass almost every day, I was not very mellow about it, taking a proprietary interest in every place I fished. One evening I arrived at a place I considered my own secret spot and there were two people fishing there. To add insult to injury, I felt, they were fly fishing, at a time when I thought I was the only one doing it. Turning purple at the wheel of my 1949 Ford, I floored the throttle and spun the steering wheel, spraying gravel on the fishermen and putting the car securely in a ditch. Looking back on those years now, I still laugh to think how far such feelings are from my current philosophy: when competition enters the sport, the sportsman departs—a statement delivered to Roderick Haig-Brown by his father.

Nevertheless, the mania of youth opened up a veritable labyrinth of places to fish, and developed a skein of knowledge which eventually resulted in the ability to apply the craft well within the limits of time and reason. In short, all that I learned has made it possible for me to fish today with relative ease, and tremendous pleasure. Now, if only there were something to fish for.

**

At six o'clock on a Saturday morning Fisherman's Wharf is the busiest neighborhood in town. While the tourists still slumber in their darkened hotel rooms, the fishermen stream in and out of bait shops and begin to gather around the docks. On the stack of one of the party boats moored across the street from the Wax Museum is a painted invitation: "Get your nibbles on the Bass Tub III." A line of eager fishermen wait to do just that. After they board, captain Cliff Anfinson assembles them on the rear deck to outline the basic system for drifting with live bait. Then, on the way to the fishing grounds, co-captain Mike sees that everyone's equipment is properly rigged.

If you wrote Anfinson into a screenplay he could be played by Ernest Borgnine, but without a space between his front teeth. Captain Cliff takes the success of his clients seriously, and advises them over and over again to pick good-looking bait out of the tank of anchovies. "Make it sexy," he tells them. The pattern is a standard one, if not entirely as simple as it seems: fish the outgoing tide at Yellow Bluff and the South Tower of the Golden Gate Bridge, then the incoming at the Rockpile just west of Alcatraz. The plan works well and by two o'clock the fishermen are back at the wharf, separating their own fish from a box crowded with big ones.

This scene is not unusual except for one thing: it is the second week in April and bass normally run at Alcatraz and the South Tower in June. No one has ever seen schools of bass there in the second week of April. These fish should currently be spawning up in the Delta country and the Sacramento River. Today, as each bass was gaffed, ripe eggs oozed out onto the deck.

No one takes this more seriously than Cliff Anfinson, and like all those who have been around fish and fishing for a lifetime, he finds it increasingly difficult to take officials, official reports, and official policies for more than what they are: reflections of the political climate camouflaged by layers of bureaucratic paperwork, confusion, duplicity and doubletalk. Anfinson is on the bay every day. He makes his living by showing people who haven't the time or the inclination to learn by themselves how to enjoy one of the Bay Area's best-wearing pleasures, striped bass fishing. When he tells you something, it's what he has seen, and it is clear that his comments and observations lack any personal ulterior motives despite his profession.

"The bay is mixed up," he confesses. "The anchovies haven't been here. The bass haven't been here. There was no fall run at all last year in Racoon Strait or at California City. Now, at the wrong time of year, suddenly there are bass where they shouldn't be. Maybe some anchovies came in and the bass followed them. I don't know. We've had a noticeable decline in the bait, the anchovies. I think too much is being taken commercially. People can't visualize what's happening. Imagine a bulldozer the size of the nets they drag in the ocean, a mile wide because that's how big those nets are. Now multiply that by fifty. Fifty bulldozers, each one a mile wide, scraping across California taking every tree, bush and animal with them. If that were to happen people would have some idea what they're doing to the ocean."

Every year the appearance of the herring in San Francisco Bay is greeted with enthusiasm by commercial fishermen, and by the press which reports on their success. More boats than ever fished the bay this year, and most took their quotas. Nonetheless, hardly anyone will argue the point that each year there are fewer and fewer fish. Herring roe is selling these days in Japan for as high as $25 a pound. According to one report, "At any one time, only about ten percent of the catch will yield roe. The rest is ground up for fertilizer, or if the fisherman can get away with it, dumped overboard. . . . By the time they'd finished, some 4,000 tons of herring were lifted from the chilly waters of the bay. . . . This year's hunt was a huge success."

Not without a hint of fatigue in his voice, Anfinson says, "They keep saying there are plenty of herring and they go on netting them as if that were true. Who knows there's enough herring? I don't think there are. Don't people remember the sardine? In Monterey they said the same thing, that there were plenty of sardines. The sardine will go on forever. They said that and went on to fish the sardines to extinction. Don't people remember that?"

Apparently not. 4,000 tons taken from San Francisco Bay alone, not counting of course what was dumped overboard when they could "get away with it." Simple arithmetic makes the bottom line 8,000,000 pounds of herring from one small bay so that Japan can have its *kazunoko*. How do you make the point? Have a few thousand pounds of herring delivered to every single office in Sacramento? Sayonara.

Generally speaking, striped bass live according to a migratory patron. In California their spawning time is from about mid-April to mid-June. Spawning doesn't begin until water temperatures reach at least fifty-eight degrees, a level which varies from year to year relative to the amount of snow runoff. And bass are essentially freshwater spawners, tolerating no more than a ration of 600 to 800 parts per million of salt to freshwater on the spawning grounds.

The migration of stripers is a rather imprecise one. After spawning, the adult fish move away from the delta and rivers into San Francisco Bay and the ocean. Exactly where they spend the summer is directly determined by the availability of food. It might be lower San Francisco Bay, the South Bay, Lower San Pablo, or outside the Gate up and down the coast from Half Moon Bay to the Russian River. When fall comes, most bass seek the inland waters where they will winter. When the water warms in the spring they will spawn again and repeat the cycle. However, this pattern is not specific, nor is it irrevocable. Not every bass follows it, and even among those which do there may be infinite varieties of both time and place.

There is no comparison possible, for instance, between striped bass and salmon. Salmon return, without exception, as a school, to the very river of their birth. There they reproduce by burying their eggs in gravel beds, and after that, again without exception, they die. Stripers will spawn wherever conditions allow. This could be in the district of their birth, or it could be in another bay or river system entirely. And rather than dig nests, bass are free spawners; they simply loose their eggs and sperm at or near the surface.

Two factors are critical to successful spawning. The first is that the eggs be allowed to float free and undamaged during the several days it takes them to hatch. Secondly, the fry must be able to survive their first and perhaps most crucial year. They must have food, namely zooplankton and neomysis shrimp. And they must have brackish water which is not too strong, the kind of mixture of fresh and saltwater normally found in the delta region.

Right now the striped bass are in very deep trouble. During the early sixties when stripers were plentiful, the total estimated population of bass larger than sixteen inches was as high as ten, possibly eleven million fish. The Department of Fish and Game estimates the current striper population at 1.5 million. That's a decline of ninety percent. The redoubtable Leon D. Adams, author of *Striped Bass Fishing in California and Oregon,* the most comprehensive analysis of the California fishery ever published, has been an observer of the bay and its bass for the last forty years. When asked to remark on the situation his answer is short and to the point. "The bass are doomed."

Before you attribute this perfectly concise remark to the symptoms

181

of old age, or something equally simplistic, keep in mind that Adams has always been one to seek proof through research. He has consistently demanded to see the pudding.

"What you keep getting from Department of Fish and Game biologists is ignorance and irresponsibility. Real research on the striped bass is lacking. When you have large bass kills as we do from time to time, these people toss off explanations which have no source in fact. As far as I can see, the fisheries projects are not aimed at truly studying the fish or their necessary environment. They are little more than thinly disguised attempts to justify projects like the Peripheral Canal so that even more water can be diverted from northern to southern California."

The average amount of water exported to San Luis Reservoir from the delta in the month of June over the past six years is almost 3.9 billion gallons per day. There is currently no firm control over existing pump valves and the amount of water being exported could be doubled. An arbitrary increase of this magnitude would reduce the already meager striper population by half, according to the Department of Fish and Game.

Marty Seldon, conservation editor for *Angler* magazine, once wrote, "It now seems crystal clear that if we approve more water conveyances like the East Side Division or the Peripheral Canal, and give the federal agencies the pump capacity to quadruple the exported water, our fishery will go to zero. You can count on it."

Because of severe drought conditions, the flow of fresh water into the delta and subsequently the bay during the normally high runoff months of May, June and July is going to be very low. Delta waters on the San Joaquin side are already too salty for stripers to spawn in, having a saline ratio of 2,700 parts per million, well above the 800 parts per million stripers can tolerate. The San Joaquin district represents as much as forty-five percent of the available spawning territory.

In spite of the fact almost half the spawning grounds are, at the moment, useless, an official with the Bay Delta Fisheries Project thought that the spawning prospects for this year looked "pretty good." I don't know. What about all those bass ready to spawn, mysteriously hanging around under the Golden Gate Bridge? Will they, as most people seem willing to believe, make an eleventh hour dash up the Sacramento River?

Or will they reabsorb their eggs and milt, and simply take a Pasadena on the whole business this year?

Even assuming that a good number of bass manage to spawn successfully in the Sacramento River and its tributaries, assurances that the progeny will survive are not forthcoming. This, in fact, is where the problem gets heavy. What has been happening, and what is likely to continue to happen, is that while we supply water for the toilets of greater Los Angeles, we are also shipping them a bonus they hadn't counted on: our striped bass.

Over the past four years, the population of juvenile striped bass in the Bay area has declined fifty percent. This is not to say they necessarily all died. Many did, but just as many took a little trip through inadequate fish screens, or past places where there should have been fish screens but weren't, and now (like so many people from somewhere else), they live in southern California.

So while there is every possibility that the stripers as we know them in San Francisco Bay are doomed, they are doing pretty well in such unlikely places as the canals and terminal reservoirs south of the Tehatchepis. Last year, fishermen caught 160,000 of them out of the San Luis-O'Neill Reservoir complex. The reason is that the large diversions have inadequate fish screens. These diversions are in the very areas where stripers spawn and the screens cannot prevent the passage of either eggs or the very small fry. A side issue is that the pumping reduces amounts of zooplankton, neomysis shrimp and benthis invertebrates which the tiny bass feed on, so even those fish which escape the pumps are adversely affected because their food supply is destroyed or shipped elsewhere.

The problems are easy to enumerate and jot down on a piece of paper, but so far they seem impossible to correct. The Department of Fish and Game does not have, and never has had, enough of a general fund to afford the personnel to handle the environmental services jobs, or for adequate enforcement. Nor have they had the money to conduct enough research on migratory fish. Add to this the fact there is no federal legislation requiring the Bureau of Reclamation to share responsibility for protecting the delta and its fishery. At the moment, the Bureau is strictly in the water export business.

In considering the problems relevant to the California striped bass fishery and its environment, we are talking about something broader and a good deal more important than just filling the leisure hours of a few people who don't know what else to do with themselves on Sunday afternoon other than go fishing. Not that there is a thing wrong with fishing on Sunday afternoons. If there were some way to measure the positive influence on the collective mental health which fishing has had on people around the Bay Area during the last seventy years, fishing would rank up there with enough food and the hugging quotient. But protecting the ecosystems is a principal priority and function of living in the twentieth century. Even if you live in Mill Valley or Tiburon, it is more important than getting rolfed or discovering your own tiny little human potential.

During this time of drought we are getting a clearer picture of how the water is distributed and where battle lines are drawn when there isn't enough to go around. But some people always knew there wasn't enough to go around, even when it was raining. These days farmers whose parents came to California during the Dust Bowl years are saying that now they may have to again pull up stakes and move for similar reasons. Pointing out there was not really enough room or water here in the first place is prying into a can of worms so long unopened even the botulism in it feels at home. The fact remains that California cannot now and never could provide the necessary resource, namely water, to support what has become a bizarre population density.

Twenty or thirty years ago precious rivers were dammed with absolute aplomb, projects that today would be bitterly fought because even a corrupt environmental impact report would be thoroughly transparent. Now we are suffering from these unsound plans and people still haven't learned from past mistakes. As you read this, the Bureau of Reclamation is spending $720,000 to see if it can find a way to divert the Klamath River for agricultural purposes. The Klamath is one of the streams included in the state Wild and Scenic Rivers Act. To give some idea what we are up against, the State Water Commission has already determined that there is sufficient ground water to meet the area's future needs, yet the Bureau has spent most of its money, while refusing to even look at ground-water supplies. Continuing to plan for more exportation of water is like buying a fishing boat so you can move to Monterey Bay and net sardines for a living. If that's not clear enough, I don't know what else to say.

Frank Bertaina with a New Zealand brown trout.

A DAY IN
PARADISE

I would call the river delicate. It flows generally to the southwest, coming out of a long, broad, arid valley to finally join a much larger river which subsequently empties into a lake. The gradient of this particular river is not at all steep. In places it riffles along, wide and shallow, then suddenly at the corner of a hayfield it will cut a high bank, turn, then move slowly and darkly through a long, deep pool. The big fish are in the pools. Three pounds is probably about average, and every day you will cast to fish of seven or eight. In a week's fishing the lucky angler will see at least one trout in the double figures.

In the vicinity of the little town of Te Anau at the southern end of the South Island where this river runs, you might easily convince yourself you are in northern California the way it was fifty years ago, Marin and Sonoma counties in particular. Part of this sensation comes from the rolling hills, gentle valleys and ample vegetation. Annual rainfall is around thirty inches, similar to that of California's wine country.

A larger part of this sense of familiarity is due to the sight and smell of the eucalyptus tree, so widely transplanted to California from New Zealand and Australia. Native Californians think of them as natural because we grew up with them; thus, oddly, seeing them in their native land makes you think of home. In the same way, New Zealanders might think of their trout as native, so important have they become to the lifestyle as well as the economy. It is hard to see this lovely island paradise without the overwhelming numbers of fish and game it now supports. But in fact, before the islands were settled by Europeans, there were no game animals and no trout.

Among the native fish are the eels, smelt, whitebait, assorted mud-fishes and bullheads and the grayling, the sole native gamefish, considered to be extinct since about 1920. The browns originally came from Europe and the rainbows from California. Brown and rainbow trout are now very widely distributed throughout both the North and South Islands, and other introduced species include Atlantic salmon, sockeye salmon, king salmon, char, Mackinaw, perch, catfish and carp.

Certain birds were native or self-introduced from Australia: the mountain parrot or Kea, herons, bitterns, paradise and grey ducks, rails, harriers and a few others. The more familiar birds, at least to North Americans, such as mallards, Canada geese, pheasants, pigeons, owls, sparrows, quail, blackbirds, thrushes, finches and sparrows, to cite a rather incomplete list, are all introduced.

Among the mammals, none of the major species now on the islands is native. As there are no predators, the deer and elk populations ballooned out of control until finally commercial hunting became necessary as a means of control. Deer are now ranched much like cattle or sheep. In spite of extensive and sophisticated market hunting, deer are still more plentiful on the South Island than in even the most remote forests of North America.

To give some perspective as to the truly rural ambience of the South Island, it is nearly the size of California, while its entire population is less than half that of the San Francisco Bay area.

One day a few years ago just before Christmas, Frank Bertaina, the ex-baseball pitcher, and I decided to walk five or six miles of the little river I was mentioning earlier. We had our friend and guide Bob Speden drop us of with an understanding he would pick us up about eight hours later at a designated place upstream.

From the road we crossed a broad meadow which stretched a thousand yards to the river. It was covered with sheep, New Zealand's principle export.

Frank smiled at me, "This is the land where men are men and the sheep are nervous."

Soon we struck the river and started upstream. The first mile was somewhat discouraging. Floods earlier in the year had altered the river's course, moving it out of its former bed so that it was now thinly spread over barren gravel. The old, scoured pools, willow-lined and deep, were stagnant and isolated from the flow. There seemed to be no place where the kind of fish we sought could find cover.

We had been having weather problems and today was no exception. Heavy rains earlier in the week had put many of the streams out of condition even though it was mid-December, the beginning of summer.

Te Anau lies immediately to the southeast of Fiordland, a steep, mountainous band of country along the west coast of the island. These rugged mountains receive vast amounts of rainfall, as much as three or four hundred inches a year, brought by storms sweeping in from the Tasman Sea. Once over the mountains in Te Anau itself, precipitation decreases dramatically to thirty inches annually, give or take ten. As Frank and I began our walk, a fair portion of the year's total seemed to be falling on us, driven into our faces by a relentless wind. Visibility was poor to impossible, no small disadvantage since the fishing here is entirely dependent upon locating and casting to individual trout. In some ways it's very much like bonefishing: seeing and stalking are as important as casting, and you can't have one without the other two.

"I try to tell people exactly what to expect down here," Frank tells me. "If they just want lots of big fish and don't particularly care how they catch them, I suggest they go to Alaska. But what you have in Southland New Zealand is not to be found anywhere else: sight fishing, one on one, with light tackle and a dry fly, for fish which will average three or four pounds, and realistically speaking, go to eight or ten."

Frank, since retiring from baseball, arranges trips for fishermen to New Zealand and is himself a consummate angler. He worries about giving his clients information which will leave them dissatisfied in the end. Strictly speaking, it is probably an expensive mistake for someone who is not at least somewhat seasoned to plan a trout fishing trip to New Zealand. Of course, you can rent a boat and go out on the lakes, troll, and catch plenty of trout. But you can do that just as easily in Minnesota or a hundred other places closer to home.

After two hours, and miles of fighting wind and rain without seeing as much as a fin, we came upon an enormous pool which Frank knew held about two-dozen fish from three to twelve pounds. We stood a long time studying the pool's broad tail, but because of the wind and glare, could not locate a trout. Then, inevitably, we spooked two big fish out of the shallows by walking by them.

At the center of the pool, close in against the far bank where the water was barely gliding, there was a dark slick. In it a fish was rising at intervals of thirty or forty seconds.

At Frank's insistence I eased out on the spacious sandbar, crouching very low until I was kneeling at the water's edge. I began to regret my choice of tackle for the day. Because of the river's small, seemingly manageable size, as well as its extreme clarity, I had brought along my favorite rod, an eight-foot Winston graphite model designed to cast a number four line, and on which I use a three. I was looking at a forty-foot cast with a long leader in a gusty side wind. Possible, but not pretty, and I tore my favorite shirt while performing the essential double haul.

The size sixteen elk-hair caddis landed right though, and as it floated over the fish, he took and I tightened. A few seconds later I gently freed the six-incher. It was the only immature trout I saw in two weeks. We never did see any of those big ones. They just weren't out feeding.

The rain eased to a miserable sprinkle so we did some hard walking to reach a series of pools which lay tight beneath gorgeous, terribly high moss-covered cliffs. In one of the pools, a dark slot where flecks of white foam passed slowly over the black water, a four-pound rainbow drifted up out of the darkness to gently sip in an insect. Frank fished to it but nothing happened. We waited.

Ten minutes later a fish rose again, this time charging two or three yards upstream in a violent rush. This fish, though, was a six- or seven-pound rainbow, an entirely different trout. I tried casting to it but with the short rod, light line, wind, and brush behind me, the fly never got near the water. The only way I could make a clear backcast for the relatively long shot needed to cover the fish was to get into the water and cast upstream. Frank advised against it but I plunged in anyway.

Just as I reached a good position and began false casting, Frank cautioned me to wait because a trout had come out into the shallows to feed actively, and it was swimming all over the place. From my low position I couldn't see under the water at all. Frank could see clearly from the bank and told me to stay very still because the fish was slowly cruising toward me. I saw it soon enough, a beautiful five-pound rainbow, and could only stand and watch helplessly as it swam past my nose and disappeared downstream, partially spooked.

"That's one of the reasons you don't want to get in the water if you can help it," Frank said with a little laugh.

The rain started up again and the sky became more closed in than ever. Frank wanted to reach three or four big pools which were still several miles upstream so we began walking at a pretty good pace. As we passed pool after delightful pool I couldn't help but be impressed with the vicissitudes of this deceptively simple stream. It is not inaccessible or remote in the least. In fact, for its whole length it runs through ranches and farms. But the sparseness of the population is easy to forget because the countryside really does look like someplace you've been before: California, as I mentioned. And in California, streams like this one were abolished years and years ago.

You forget how little time and pressure it takes to change the fragile essence of nature. For instance, as recently as fifteen years ago, the much-vaunted Armstrong Spring Creek, only ten minutes away from my front door in Montana, was a wild, seldom fished jewel of a stream. Five or six years ago, the late Dan Bailey told me he couldn't bear to go there anymore because of what had been done by thoughtless landowners and a healthy cross section of the angling public. Today, the stream is badly overfished, its banks so heavily trod that in places the vegetation refuses to grow back. This once free-flowing stream full of large, wild fish, is now changed, channeled and dammed. Its banks have been ruthlessly stripped of vegetation, and hatchery rainbows have been carelessly released. While some large fish do remain, the trout are generally smallish and nearly all have been caught and released at least once. And it now costs thirty dollars a day to fish Armstrong's.

Trout Unlimited tried to protect it, but when a stream reaches the point where it requires protection, it is already too late. I don't want to be misunderstood: trying to preserve and protect Armstrong Creek was certainly admirable, and obviously, necessary. But by that time, which was several years ago, what had made the stream famous and legendary among fly fishermen remained only as a myth. Its wildness is gone forever, and the fisherman is no longer free on its banks.

I thought about this as Frank and I were walking along what was so obviously a wild yet accessible river. What essentially destroys wildness? The answer is obvious: pressure. We walked through many farms yet saw no farmers. We walked on and crossed a number of roads but saw few cars. Nor did we ever encounter other fishermen, not only on this day, on this river, but in three weeks on three-dozen rivers. One excellent pool flowed by what appeared to be a gravel company, but the equipment looked unused and no one was around. There you have it: no one was around.

Of course, to be fair, the fishing in this little stream, especially with the water as low and clear as it was, is simply not for the occasional fisherman. A guy with a Saturday off, throwing a two-ounce Devon spoon on fifteen-pound line, is merely going to put the trout under the banks for a while. And a clumsy fly caster will do likewise.

Presently, we came to a substantial pool with a high clay bank rising steeply on the outside of the curve. The tailout was perhaps a hundred feet wide, coming up very slowly so that its mean depth was about a foot. Beneath the high bank at the center of the pool, the water was seven or eight feet deep, slow, dark and promising.

We looked cautiously over the rim. The rain had stopped and the wind had let up, but the skies were still dark in what was now late afternoon. The tailout was so shallow that most of it was transparent. Right away, Frank spotted a brown of at least seven pounds nymphing in about ten inches of water on the far side.

"Look at this." He nudged me.

Another brown, clearly several pounds larger than the first, was slowly cruising down out of the deeper water. It passed the first fish, and moved into the shallowest part of the tail where we lost it in the glare.

"Go ahead," I said.

"No way. Go around and try them. I'll spot."

Walking downstream, I crossed in the fast water well below where we'd last seen the biggest brown. Upon reaching the beach, I stayed back away from the pool until opposite Frank, then I crawled right to the shallow edge.

"Look," I heard Frank say softly. Upstream I could see the heavy rings. With the wind down, a big fish had taken something off the top.

"Okay now," Frank directed. "The bigger brown we saw come out of the pool is slowly working up toward you. He's taking nymphs every ten or fifteen seconds."

I checked my fly and leader: a size sixteen dark impressionistic weighted nymph on 5x. If only a nagging wife had been there to tell me how stupid I was I might have gone to something more stout and sensible. As it was, I kept thinking about the still, shallow, crystal-clear water and stuck with the fool's choice. I made the cast as Frank directed, across stream and slightly down. The current pulled the line around slowly and I stripped in a bit so the fly would swing in front of the trout.

"Retrieve," Frank said. "He just took something."

He had just taken something all right, namely my fly. I came up gently and felt him for about one second, but the 5x leader had been reduced to no x by false casting or whatever, the biggest trout I'd ever hooked sprinted for deep water with a tiny fly in his lip.

Upstream another fish rose. "I'll go to a dry fly and try that one," I said, hoping to overcome total mortification and disappointment. Frank moved up and cautiously looked over the edge just as the fish rose again. "It's a beautiful male rainbow. A good one too. Six or seven pounds."

The water was now extremely calm. Frank was silhouetted against the sky. Below him the cliff was almost orange in the fading light. Against it, the water drifted slowly, a blackish green, with just a few flecks of white foam to indicate its speed. The trout rose again.

I had to make a decision. I pulled out the 4x spool; there was only about a foot left on it so I took some new 5x. While these fish are not particularly selective, they are touchy, and the first shot has to be a good one. I put the elk-hair caddis back on, greased it a little, and started working out line for a fifty-foot cast. I was kneeling, and it was all I could do to control so much line. But the loops stayed open and suddenly the fly appeared on the water, shining like a light. The drift seemed endless, moving slowly by me.

Frank saw the big rainbow elevate. Then I saw its substantial jaws come out of the water, and I let them disappear before easing back. There was no resistance and the trout was gone.

"What the hell happened this time?" Frank called. "He took it perfectly."

"I know he did. I thought I gave him time."

I flipped a backcast and caught the leader, bringing the fly up close. The tippet had fouled under the hair wing so that the leader was pulling the fly backward, making it impossible to hook a fish. I felt like a frustrated child, very much wanting to snap the rod into numerous small sections. Instead, I screamed an inner scream and slumped onto the muddy beach.

"Wait a minute," Frank said. "Another fish just rose up above."
He walked up the bluff and looked over. "It's another rainbow, a female, not as big as the other one but still a good five pounds."

Pulling myself together, I crawled into position, checked the tippet
for knots and tied on a fresh fly. I did what I could to keep the loops
tangle-free, putting a clean point on the delivery, and once again the
fly landed just right. It drifted slowly, the trout rose and took it. Resistance! After a bit of furious head shaking the rainbow made a smok-
ing run upstream, taking the entire fly line and ten yards of backing in
a matter of five or six seconds. It was a big pool and all I had to do
was keep a light but steady hand.

Frank called from across the way, "There are some big rocks up
there where the fish is."

A fair warning, but the leader was already broken.

In order to reach the road and our ride a couple of miles away,
we needed to start moving. I felt drained. The last hour had been a
kind of emotional roller coaster; I'd hooked, or at least had takes from,
the three largest trout of my life right in succession. I was disappointed
and embarrassed at my own clumsiness, yet at the same time there was
also a sense of exhilaration, and even in a perverse and perhaps incomplete way, accomplishment. These weren't exactly minnows and it had
taken all day just to locate them. Had things gone even a hair differently
I might now be able to give you the weights and lengths of three huge
trout, even though I had no intention of killing any of them. As it is,
I have a very thrilling and precise memory to carry with me forever.

The last thing I remember about that day is that it rained very
hard on us all the way back.

Del Brown about to board the helicopter.

UP OVER
AND DOWN UNDER

The DeHavilland Beaver was rapidly losing what little altitude it had gained to begin with, and over the pilot's shoulder we could just barely see the tiny Eskimo village of Goodnews, and beyond it, the terrific expanse of the Bering Sea. As the DeHavilland's wheels touched down on the gravel strip, the four of us were more than anxious to get out. Ever since boarding an hour-and-a-half earlier at the little town of Dillingham, about three-hundred miles west of Anchorage, we'd been mercilessly wedged between far too much luggage and too many fishing rod cases.

We bounced to a stop at a beach crowded with derelict boats. Leaning here and there against them were a number of Eskimo men, while Eskimo teenagers raced around on three-wheel all-terrain vehicles. There were boats moored in the harbor too, and pulled up on the beach was our transportation upriver: three fourteen-foot aluminum skiffs.

We climbed out and got right to the business of transferring our gear for a week's fishing into the boats. When we'd finished, one of the guides, a young man who introduced himself as Dave, approached me.

"Are you Russ Chatham?"

"Yes I am." We shook hands.

"I have a message for you."

"You do?" Fear surged through my body. How did anyone know where I was? In every sense of the word, we were exactly in the middle of nowhere. It had taken days to reach this sanctuary from telephones and charity requests. My God, I thought, my entire family's been wiped out in a huge California earthquake, and they've wired in the news on

197

the very first day of a vacation in Alaska that I've been looking forward to all year.

"Yes. The message is from two girls in Australia."

"What! I don't know anybody in Australia."

Dave smiled. "Sure you do. Well, not really. Not yet anyway. The message is, 'Great. We'd love it. We're planning a trip to the States next summer.'"

"I don't get it."

"I was down in New Zealand last winter and walked around the country some. Think about it."

Mainly, I was relieved that my loved ones had not been crushed beneath tons of rubble in an encore of the fire and earthquake of 1906. San Francisco was safe. I'd solve the mystery later; right now it was raining like hell, and cold, so I huddled in the bow of the skiff as we started the run to camp. The cold, damp weather made my knee hurt, a dull pain right in the joint. I stretched it, rubbed it, and thought about the enigmatic message. As I massaged the aching knee, I suddenly understood what Dave meant and tipped my head back and laughed out loud. The freezing gale took the laugh and hurled it off into nowhere. Our Eskimo boatman, standing in the rear of the skiff, looked at me and smiled.

It had been a year since I'd returned from New Zealand. I'd gone there for the trout fishing, and hadn't been disappointed. I happen to live in Livingston, Montana, a town the Chamber of Commerce calls "The Trout Capitol of the World."

Now, I love Livingston, and there certainly is plenty of wonderful trout fishing nearby. But, comparatively speaking, you're talking about the five waitresses at Martin's 24-hour café up against a crowded Sunday afternoon at the Playboy Mansion West.

The thing which struck me first and foremost, aside from the beauty of the countryside, the countless rivers and their plethora of enormous trout, was the distinct feeling of having been flung backward in time. In Montana it would be, say, forty years ago, in California, sixty or seventy. Low population densities and a relatively low amount of racial, economic, or civic strife, all combine to create a society without tension or neuroses, where no one hurries, and everyone is polite. It's like Tahiti with British accents and snow.

There is, of course, a downside to this apparent heaven. The cuisine, or rather cooking, is perfectly awful. And the culture seems somewhat watery. There is a lack of night life, not to mention café society glitter and wit. But if that's what you want, don't fly around the world; go to New York and take a cab to Elaine's.

As soon as we arrived, nasty weather tormented my friends and I. The wind blew, it rained, and low, gray skies hid the mountains from view. Finally, many of the streams colored up. We had been waiting for a break in the weather to reach several of the South Island's more remote streams: the Clinton, the Worsley, and the Greenstone. Finally, we decided to simply go ahead and plan a day on the Greenstone regardless of weather. One of our guides, the late Fred Gill, arranged for a helicopter to pick us up at a clearing along the Eglinton River some miles north of Te Anau.

"Be there and ready at nine a.m. Have your rods taken down, hold tight to your hat, and don't go near the tail of the machine," Fred advised with a small smile. "This chap's a deer hunter and he won't be wanting to waste a bit of time. And when he tells you where and when to be for the pickup to come out, you'd best be there or you'll spend the night outside."

Four of us were going out that day. We found the clearing and checked our gear. About ten minutes later we saw the chopper coming in and felt as if we'd entered a *M.A.S.H.* episode. The helicopter made a no-nonsense landing and the pilot motioned us over. We ran to the cockpit and crawled in. Moments later we rose, tilted forward, and headed up the Eglinton. A Hughes 500 like the one we rode in can make a ground speed of 125 miles per hour and we were clipping along at about that pace, not far from the steep, beech-forested mountains on either side of us.

The torque and centrifugal force were tremendous as we negotiated the canyon, swinging to and fro around each switchback. There were no seat belts and the flimsy canvas door wouldn't hold a Barbie Doll. Sitting on the floor, the fingers of my left hand were wedged into an unseen crack underfoot and my right hand grasped an overhead strap. Think *Guiness Book of World Records* white knuckles. It took about twenty minutes to climb up the headwaters of the Eglinton, brush over the craggy divide, and begin our descent into the upper reaches of the famous Greenstone. What had begun as a terrifying odyssey toward sure death by being fired from the ship on a sharp turn, like a ball bearing out of a slingshot, had now become high adventure. Talk about getting away from the tourists.

The helicopter pulled up and settled on a grassy bluff above the river. I crawled out with Del Brown, my fishing partner for the day.

"See you at five o'clock just above the gorge," the pilot said. The chopper rose and banked sharply, taking the other two anglers upstream. Thirty seconds later we couldn't see or hear it anymore.

The wind shrieked down the river valley at a velocity of at least thirty knots. Del and I walked to the water. We could tell it was quite high, although clear.

"What do you think, Del?"

"I don't know. We'll never be able to spot any fish with the river up like it is, the sky so dark and the wind so strong."

"Maybe we should've stayed with the aircraft."

"C'mon. We'll just fish likely water with streamers and nymphs."

At the first good pool a large fish swirled behind Del's fly but didn't get hooked. The wind freshened and became so fierce we had difficulty walking against it. On this section of river, the pools weren't very well defined, so we decided to move on until we hit something promising.

In about two miles we came to some steep cliffs, and were forced to skirt inland around them. We ended up high above the river, looking down on an undercut bank. There was no way to fish the pool properly from our side, but it looked as though one could get upstream from the cutbank (a very narrow slot, actually), make a cast straight downstream and pay out line a few inches at a time until the fly had insinuated itself through all of the best looking water.

"Think that will work, Del?" I asked after delivering the explanation.

"Try it. I'll watch from up here."

I slid down the steep, grassy slope, reached a rock at the head of the cut, made a short cast right downstream, and began jigging the fly a little, gradually letting it out a foot or two at a time. It didn't seem to be right somehow, but I kept at it until seventy or eighty feet of line stretched down into the pool.

Del yelled from the cliff just as the pull came. He'd seen the trout rush from beneath the cutbank, flash and take. The fish went berserk, jumping crazily, taking more and more line down into the center of the pool. I ran up the cliff toward Del to recover line, but the trout persisted in surging itself against the far shore. In the high wind, the orange fly line billowed out in a huge arc like a spinnaker sail. It was impossible to direct the trout at all, so strong was its resistance. I had to be careful, too, of the added pressure applied by the wind; the fish was nearly a hundred feet away and most of that line was in the air.

Directly across from us part of the river broke off into a side channel, not large, but flowing enough for the trout to push implacably toward it. Slithering through the narrow opening, getting what current there was behind him, the fish made it into the first pool of the channel. Now the whole fly line was completely out, in addition to fifty or sixty feet of backing.

Del laughed a little. "That's the damnedest thing I ever saw."

The trout kept going from pool to pool until at last he stopped, well over a hundred yards away from us. The orange fly line had disappeared completely down the channel by now. To my advantage, the much thinner micron backing didn't billow quite so spectacularly in the wind.

"Damn," I said looking at Del, and started to laugh. "He's got everything but the rod and reel. If I lose my fly line I can't fish anymore today. Tell you what. You hold the rod and I'll go upstream to a place where I can cross, then I'll pick up the line over there. When I do, you secure the reel handle with this rubber band that's around the reel seat, then throw the outfit into the river and I'll pull it over."

"You sure? If something breaks you'll lose that priceless little Bogdan reel, not to mention the Winston rod."

"I'll be careful."

About three-hundred yards upstream a fast riffle tailed out a bit and it looked like the only possible crossing. I was wearing leather wading shoes with non-slip felt soles and a pair of coveralls. Oddly, in spite of the season—it was mid-December, early summer in New Zealand—and the cold rainy weather, I waded wet in the river without too much discomfort.

Crossing, though, that was a different matter. When I neared midstream the water was more than waist deep and very fast. It was also cold; the family jewels retreated with a vengeance. My camera was in a chest pocket, and I feared this was going to develop into a swim. By just a hair it didn't, although I got soaked up to my armpits. I was across, and that's what mattered.

When I got out into the brisk whistling wind, things began to really cool off. I clambered over the uneven terrain until I was at last opposite Del and had my backing in hand.

"Toss it!"

Del hesitated, then pitched a thousand dollars worth of irreplaceable tackle into the turbulent current. I eased it over and put my hands on it. Quickly reeling up the line, I followed it down the channel until the fly line came back through the guides and I finally found the trout, holding still in the current. He exploded out of the water when I pressured him, turned, and took the fly line again as I ran stiffly after him. I was shivering hard now; my feet and hands were nearly numb.

I had thought it would be a relatively simple matter to land the trout—or lose it—once I was over on the side channel. This did not prove to be the case, as the fish fought hard, working its way steadily downstream until we neared the main river. I found the thought of the trout getting out into the strong current again perfectly appalling, so I applied Devil May Care pressure. In a moment the trout was on the gravel.

It was a magnificent rainbow of about six pounds and as silver as a steelhead fresh out of the ocean. I pulled out my pocket camera and took a picture of it on the beach beside the fly rod, then slipped it back into the river, holding it upright until it sidled away. By this time I was barely functional from cold, but felt it was important to get back across the river to join Del. Stumbling back up the quarter of a mile, I looked at the point of my earlier crossing and decided to try farther upstream. I quickly found a good place to try, but as I stepped near the edge of a seven foot drop, the lip of the bank sloughed off and I went plummeting into the water below. It was shallow, but I still got wet up to my neck. Worse than that, I landed on my left knee among a pile of submerged boulders. The pain shot up my leg, and that, plus near hypothermia, put me close to blacking out. I somehow climbed out of the water and sat down on the bank. I was terribly dizzy but still aware of Dell yelling from across the river. I think I tried to call back that I was fine.

The possibility of missing the helicopter ride home crossed my mind and I forced myself to stand. We couldn't really hear one another over the combined roar of the river and wind, so I motioned Del to go upstream. I made myself walk, and although it hurt to do so, I covered some ground. With the aid of a wading staff Del crossed at a wide place in the river about a mile upstream. I sat down and waited for him, hoping that he wouldn't slip. I was not in any condition to rush to his aid.

"You all right?" he asked when he finished crossing.

"I think so. At first I was a little worried, but I can walk even though it hurts."

"From clear across the river I could see your face go white as a sheet. Sure you'll be okay?"

"I know I will. Why don't you try this big pool while I sit down out of the wind for a while. I'm really cold."

Being out of the driving wind felt good and I stretched the leg and watched Del fish. It wasn't long before he hooked a trout as beautiful as the one I'd caught earlier. The difference was that while it gave him a great battle, he didn't let it nearly kill him.

The bottom of the gorge was a couple of miles away and after Del fished through the pool, we headed out. Once there we sat down out of the wind, had a sandwich, and drank some hot tea from our thermos. It tasted wonderful, but I was soaked to the skin from toes to neckline and had begun to think hysterical thoughts.

About a mile above us, nestled against the treeline, we could see a small cabin. The government locates such cabins along hiking trails and you can reserve one for the night by planning ahead. As we ate I longingly watched the house.

"Think there's firewood in there, Del?"

"I don't know. Probably. I understand when you stay at the cabins you're supposed to replace anything you use. Must include firewood, don't you think?"

"Look. Isn't that someone on the porch?"

"Seems to be. Two people I think."

I became obsessed with the idea of a hot fire. I was so cold that I started thinking something bad might happen. According to Del's watch it was still about three hours until helicopter time, and frankly, it was an ugly day for fishing.

"Tell you what I think I'm going to do. You don't have to come along although you're more than welcome. I'm going to walk up there and see about avoiding death by freezing."

"Sure, I'll go. Fishing in this kind of weather isn't my idea of fun."

It took us nearly thirty minutes to get to the cabin. Halfway there we could make out the people putting on knapsacks. Then they stepped off the porch and disappeared into the woods.

We finally arrived and went inside, where there was indeed a wood stove and plenty of firewood. I lost no time in getting it blazing. In the cupboard were matches, tea, coffee and an assortment of canned foods. If you were lost, stranded, or soaking wet, this place could save your life. I draped my wet clothes around the hot stove and stood as close to it as possible without blistering the skin on my behind. From the cabin's large sliding glass doors we had a spectacular view of the upper and lower Greenstone valleys and the gorge. It looked like we could hike the latter in thirty minutes. Oddly, my knee hurt but not so much when the pressure of walking was applied. I no longer feared missing our ride.

"Hey, look at this," Del said, holding up what looked like a ledger. "It's a guest book. Everyone who's been here in the past year or so has signed it and left some notes about their trip. It's a wonder there's a fish left in the river; seems like every one of them not only caught one, but elected to grill it right here where we sit."

I still hadn't thawed out yet, so while Del thumbed through the book reading me parts of the more interesting entries, I huddled by the stove and stared absently at its inconsequential design as if it were a religious shrine.

"Oh boy!" Del exclaimed after reading in silence for some minutes. "Here, you better read this one yourself."

The latest entry indicated that two young female hikers from Australia had arrived at the cabin last evening. To their vast disappointment, no male hikers were present. Their dismay was recorded in the guest book in excruciating detail. Modesty prevents me from quoting those purple passages. Suffice it to say the tongue loomed large in their musings about what might feel good after a day of hard walking. As they wrote on, electronic devices and turgid members were also mentioned fondly.

Now, we had been fishing for a couple of weeks, and having a splendid time of it. But with regard to the meeting of women for the purpose of conversation, friendship and sex, well, one simply had to, as they say, put it on the back burner. One could have more profitably looked for the crown jewels along a curb in the East Village.

My first impulse was to run after them along the trail, and I might have done it if I hadn't been crippled and half frozen to death. So it was then that I penned my reply. In short, I promised them the moon if they ever visited America. And to demonstrate my utter sincerity in the matter, I carefully and legibly left my address, telephone number and a highly detailed map of where I live. Call collect anytime, I said.

When my clothes were fairly dry I got back into them. We put out the fire and left the cabin for our rendezvous with technology. When we reached the gorge we stopped to rest a minute.

"Ships passing in the night," I said dreamily.

"What."

"Ships passing in the night. It's a great metaphor when you picture it literally, isn't it?"

Minutes later we could hear the deep hammering of the helicopter as it came to retrieve us.

205